1-736

TIME HUNTER

PECULIAR LIVES

TIME HUNTER

PECULIAR LIVES
by PHILIP PURSER-HALLARD

First published in England in 2005 by Telos Publishing Ltd
61 Elgar Avenue, Tolworth, Surrey, KT5 9JP, England - www.telos.co.uk
Telos Publishing Ltd values feedback. Please e-mail us with any comments
you may have about this book to: feedback@telos.co.uk

ISBN: 1-903889-47-2 (paperback)
Peculiar Lives © 2005 Philip Purser-Hallard.
ISBN: 1-903889-48-0 (deluxe hardback)
Peculiar Lives © 2005 Philip Purser-Hallard.
Time Hunter format © 2003 Telos Publishing Ltd. Honoré Lechasseur and
Emily Blandish created by Daniel O'Mahony.
The moral rights of the author have been asserted.

Typeset by Arnold T. Blumberg
& ATB Publishing Inc. (www.atbpublishing.com)

Printed in India

1 2 3 4 5 6 7 8 9 10 11 12 13 14 15

THE TIME HUNTER

Honoré Lechasseur and Emily Blandish … Honoré is a black American ex-GI, now living in London, 1950, working sometimes as a private detective, sometimes as a 'fixer', or spiv. Now life has a new purpose for him as he has discovered that he is a time-sensitive. In theory, this attribute, as well as affording him a low-level perception of the fabric of time itself, gives him the ability to sense the whole timeline of any person with whom he comes into contact. He just has to learn how to master it.

Emily is a strange young woman whom Honoré has taken under his wing. She is suffering from amnesia, and so knows little of her own background. She comes from a time in Earth's far future, one of a small minority of people known as time channellers, who have developed the ability to make jumps through time using mental powers so highly evolved that they could almost be mistaken for magic. They cannot do this alone, however. In order to achieve a time-jump, a time channeller must connect with a time-sensitive.

When Honoré and Emily connect, the adventures begin.

DEDICATION

To B, with all my love.

'In the stars' view, no doubt, these creatures were mere vermin;
yet each to itself, and sometimes one to another,
was more real than all the stars.'
Olaf Stapledon, *Star Maker*, 1937.

'I have looked pretty carefully into lots of minds, big and little, and it's devastatingly clear to me that in big matters *Homo sapiens* is a species with very slight educable capacity. He has entirely failed to learn his lesson from the last war.'
Olaf Stapledon, *Odd John*, 1935.

'In fact, given sufficient biological knowledge and eugenical technique, it might be possible to breed new human types of men to people the planets [...] the work might start with experiments on some Equatorial varieties of our species.'
Olaf Stapledon, address to the British Interplanetary Society, 1948.

CONTENTS

FOREWORD

by the Author, Erik Clevedon

Readers of my earlier book, *The Peculiar*, will recognise in the current volume the sequel and conclusion to its remarkable story. Like *The Peculiar*, *Peculiar Lives* is not fiction, but a true chronicle, in which some of the names and locations have alone been altered. In recounting incidents at which I was not myself present, I have endeavoured to stay as true as possible to the accounts given me by the real individuals involved; rarely I have permitted myself a novelist's licence, and on all such occasions I have remained as faithful as I am able to the spirit of events, if not their letter.

I am aware that to some readers these statements will seem outlandish. To maintain that *The Peculiar* and *Peculiar Lives* are true accounts is to claim a historical status for persons and happenings surely more suited to the lurid fantasies which come to us in magazine form from the far side of the Atlantic. After all, even the late Mr Wells, in presenting us with the scientific possibility of travelling through time, restrained himself from any pretence that his whimsical account was the truth.

I have not Mr Wells' advantages, however. I not only know that time-travel is possible, but have seen its effects with my own eyes; I have been in direct, if mostly unwitting, contact with a being from the distant future; I know the truth that there have walked among human beings as innocuous as myself, individuals whose abilities are so potent that our feeble species should tremble at their footsteps. I know how these creatures came to exist, and I know the lengths to which our worldly authorities will go to end their existences if they may.

I am older now than my sixty-four years, and my novels are largely neglected; my ideas, more important to me by far than the sprawling tales in which I have presented them, almost universally ignored. When I add that the recent experiences of which I write confirm that my *other* stories (*The Coming Times*, *Men of the Times*, *The Star Beasts*) have also been, if not absolutely true, then at least inspired and guided by a mind beyond and far superior to my own, I will doubtless be spurned as a ranting madman.

No matter. I fear I will not be required to endure the kindly scorn of my critics for much longer. I set this chronicle before you now, as a true account of the events which transpired in the summer of 1950, involving the young woman named Emily Blandish, her unique associate Honoré Lechasseur, young Percival 'the peculiar' and myself. Treat it as a fantasy if you will, but a fantasy which embodies, like all the best of its kind, certain truths about reality.

In the end, that is all I am entitled to ask.

E C
London, 1950.

1. EMILY AND VIOLET

A superior young woman, Emily Blandish exhibited a childlike frailty of frame with which her womanly independence of mind contested ceaselessly and sternly. Her large round eyes, which were sea-green, beheld the world with a weary determination, yet on occasion betrayed in her the innocent bewilderment of a child. For this there was good reason.

For all that those who met her took away an impression of a woman who knew her own mind, Emily had mislaid most of hers some time before. You may recall the case, which was a celebrated one in London for a while. An amnesiac young woman, clad in only the flimsiest of nightwear, Emily had emerged from the fog and shadows of the East End in late 1949 only to collapse into a policeman's arms, her mind a tablet whose contents had been wiped clean away. Her antecedents had never been established; so far as I know, her lost memories remain missing to this day.

She had not allowed this unusual handicap to cripple her, however. For some time now she had been engaged in philanthropic work of a somewhat esoteric nature, in conjunction with a partner as unique and gifted as herself.

When Emily Blandish entered St Pancras Station on a cool morning of June 1950, her thoughts, as often, were on this matter of her vanished past. Her light brown hair, worn long, hung loose about her shoulders, and she sported a light summer overcoat. She was bound

13

that day for a certain office in North London, where she was to make contact with a business associate, the details of whose affairs shall not be of concern to us.

Something in the quality of light in that morning's chilly air had put her in mind of that white radiance which formed her earliest, uncomprehended recollection: a light which shone so brightly that it might abolish darkness forever, given only sufficient time to blaze forth unextinguished. Often she felt that all she did towards the aid of others was directed at no other end than bringing them to that light, or it to them. Sometimes indeed (and with a lack of unwarranted humility which was typical of her) she considered herself in the light of the *bodhisattva* of Eastern legend, returned to Earth from that serene illumination of non-being which the Buddhists call *nirvana* to guide others through the murky gloom of reality. In darker moments, she feared that she was driven by the vanished memory of some guilt for which she must atone.

It was with reluctance that Emily focused her attention back on her mundane surroundings: the pressing crowd whose warmth held back the morning's chill, the smells of smoke and engine-oil, the ticket queue requiring her attendance. The time was shortly before nine o'clock, and the great Victorian concourse teemed with Londoners about their daily business like a droplet of blood beneath a microscope. Each individual, a corpuscle swept along the city's bloodstream from her arterial railways into the capillaries of her streets and alleys, had his function in that greater organism's life; yet each had too his own concerns and cares and petty vanities, of vivider significance to him than any belonging to the vaster body.

While her senses descended to the reality of the lives surrounding her, Emily became aware of something out of place. It was, she would later tell me, 'not anything shocking – something very subtle, hiding away in the corner of my eye, or my mind'. She compared the experience to 'one of those pictures where something's not quite as it should be – there's something missing, or something there that isn't right. It takes a moment to see what it is, but once you have it you can't ever look at that picture again in the same way'.

She sensed, rather than saw, that there was something moving through the crowd. Of course there were many such things, each one a human being like herself; but this one was different. She felt it as an absence, a travelling emptiness in that bustle of humanity like the ever-shifting eye of a tempest. If she looked at it hard out of the corner of her eye, she could nearly see it for what it was; and then she got the trick of it, and the out-of-place thing stood visibly before her.

It was a young girl, as she appeared, of indeterminate age, strolling at leisure through the station's concourse. The mob seethed unheeding past her, like a river parting on either side of a rock; while this child, with deft hands and a sly expression, relieved its every tenth or twelfth member of a wallet, purse or watch. These she crammed into a leather clutch-bag which looked to have itself been stolen. As far as Emily could make out there was no reason for the victims of these thefts not to remark her darting eyes and agile hands; nonetheless, they passed by her unheeding.

An instant after she was observed, the pickpocket looked up in startlement. Emily was strongly impressed by the fact that, instead of casting around to see who had perceived her, the girl glanced towards Emily directly, for all the world as if Emily had cried out upon a silent hillside. At once the child turned and plunged away through the crowd. Abandoning for the moment all notion of a ticket, Emily left the queue and hurried after her.

It was a queer pursuit. Emily kept the girl in sight as she struggled through the throng: the young thief seemed able to part the multitude ahead of her, and thus was able always to proceed without impediment, while Emily had to push between its members in the usual way. The girl's gait was peculiar, almost bestial, putting Emily in mind of the undulation of a lemur. Still, the child was slightly lame in one leg, and her pursuer, who was in the prime of physical health, was able several times to narrow the distance between them.

When this happened the fugitive, who was casting worried looks backward at Emily, would pause abruptly, and gaze shrewdly into her eyes. At these times Emily would find to her discomfiture that her attention wandered: she would remember her appointment with a start, and turn back towards the ticket queue; or be struck suddenly by the morning light seeping through the station's canopy, or by the smell of hot food. The girl would use this opportunity to make up her speed, until Emily recollected herself and resumed her pursuit.

She told me afterwards, 'It was like a dream – one of the ones where it's vitally important you find something, or do something, and yet you get distracted by absurd trifles. And all the while the thing you're really after is receding further and further into the distance. Does everyone have dreams like that, Erik, or is it only me?' I believe that this talent of Violet's (for that was the young thief's name) acted by establishing a resonance between her own mental vibrations and those in the region of Emily's brain wherein these dreams were generated, producing a like mental state in waking life.

From the glimpses she was permitted, Emily thought the pickpocket's stature similar to her own; yet her quarry was proportioned something like an eight-year-old, with a large head and short limbs. Beneath the rather scant brown hair her cranium was very large, and protruded oddly in a dome behind. Her eyes were huge, her right bright blue, her left the startling violet for which she had been named; and her mouth, at odds with her childlike appearance, was full and sensuous. She was attired in serviceable, unpretentious clothing, which had a hand-made appearance to it.

Emily had by now convinced herself that this strange urchin, thief or no, was of importance to her own perennial and enigmatic mission. As yet the justification for this baffled her, yet she felt it with conviction. It was with some alarm, therefore, that she saw the child, still glancing back towards her, run pell-mell into a brace of policemen standing by the station's nearest entrance. It was plain that the constables, unlike the others in that crowd, had perceived the fugitive as well as her pursuer: perhaps, Emily thought, their professional interest or training had rendered them less susceptible to whatever influence was being exerted on those others present.

At all events the girl's flight was unceremoniously arrested, as moments later she was herself. Emily was surprised, and increasingly alarmed, to see the escapee tripped by one of the constables as she attempted to tear past them, whereupon his colleague drew his truncheon and smacked her smartly as she fell, at the rear of her malformed skull.

A moment later he was hauling her to her feet and passing her limp frame over to his partner; then he directed his attention towards Emily herself, who had only now succeeded in reining in her headlong rush. 'Could you come here a minute, please, miss?' he asked courteously.

'Why are you hurting that girl?' she asked him in indignation, for when the young pickpocket had been lying on the floor, clearly unconscious, the man's companion had aimed a vicious kick at the child's lean ribs. Emily could see him now, dragging the helpless figure away with little care or gentleness.

'Now now, miss, she's only getting what's coming to her,' the first policeman replied. 'The girl's a thief.' His tone was genial.

'Yes, but –' She wanted to protest that policemen did not beat up young girls; not even in London, and not even when they were thieves. But it was evident that the girl was no ordinary thief: perhaps her persecutors were not ordinary policemen. She said: 'Yes, but I think she's hurt. Her leg –'

'You just leave that up to us, miss,' the man said in what he considered to be a reassuring tone. His face was sharp and brutal, with something oddly flat about the eyes; he looked a man who would rarely take offence, but might pretend to do so with great violence if it suited him. He stood far outside the usual conception of a police constable, and even outside the expectations of Emily, whose experiences with the police had not invariably been congenial. 'What we're looking for,' he said, 'is her accomplice.'

'Accomplice?' Emily said. She wondered if the man was trying to trap her into giving evidence against the girl; but she recalled, dismayed, that she had already assented to the proposition that the child was a thief. 'There wasn't an accomplice,' she insisted. 'I saw her. She was working alone.' Covertly she peered at the policeman's uniform, trying to discern his number, but there was none visible. She saw that he wore two pieces of unfamiliar equipment over his ears. These extended up into his helmet, and she wondered if they were a new form of police radio, for communicating with the police station. (From where she might have gained such an idea I cannot say, a wireless receiver being a rather bulky piece of equipment, but such was her conjecture.)

'We'll have to take a statement from you, miss.' The constable took her into a waiting room, for which he bullied a station porter into handing him the keys. Locked inside with him, Emily made out a summary of the events which she had witnessed, eliding the less explicable aspect of the girl's crimes. She made the child out to be no more than a skilful pickpocket, and herself to be unusually observant. Steeling herself, she gave a false address and the name 'Joan Barton'.

She had intended to emphasise in her statement the brutal actions of the two police constables, but found herself cowed by the officer's flat eyes. She omitted them, despising herself.

This formality concluded, the man seemed keenly interested in the thief's supposed accomplice. 'Are you sure you didn't see him, miss?' he asked. 'We've got some good descriptions, from witnesses who was sure they were working together. He'd be a queer one to look at, same as her – kind of foreign-like, thin and lithe with a big head. Great big green eyes, black hair in little curls like a nigger. Probably dressed same as her, too.'

Emily had seen no such person, and insisted so. At length, and with reluctance, the policeman unlocked the waiting-room and let her go. 'You watch yourself, miss,' he told her, with definite but undirected menace. 'There's some funny people about. And if you see that young man we been speaking of, you give me a call, all right?' He had passed her a calling-card bearing a telephone number and the name of 'PC Grayles', supposedly of Lancing Street Police Station. Emily was fairly certain that there was no such establishment.

By now she had missed her train, and practically her appointment itself. Finding a public box she telephoned her apologies to her intended contact, who was displeased with her, and expressed himself upon this theme at some length. This conversation concluded, Emily inserted the money for a second call, but reconsidered when she saw an aimless-looking man waiting outside the box for her to finish. She pushed the button to return her money instead, and left the telephone box and the station, taking several buses and an intentionally circuitous route back to her rooms. Once home, she made the telephone call.

What became of the young pilferer Violet and her captors, and how Emily became once again embroiled in her story, I will tell shortly. Meanwhile, I must begin to recount my own part in these events, and therefore give some details of how I occupied myself, the evening of that same day.

2. MYSELF AND PERCIVAL

I had been working, with no great degree of enthusiasm, on an article for one of our more sententious national newspapers; one of the few whom my credentials as a novelist and philosopher still suffice to impress. The substance of my remarks, as so often in recent years, concerned the current imperfection and future perfectibility of mankind.

If this is a subject to which I find myself returning frequently, and ever more urgently, as my days as a member of that remarkable species draw to a close, it is because for the first time in man's short history he really and surely holds in his hands the power to achieve, not merely his survival, but his betterment. If I myself am not to persist, it is of grave importance to me to know that my descendants and those of their generation should do so, and should become more closely and more competently suited to their role as guardians and protectors of this planet.

The great wars of this century, and other atrocities of recent memory, reveal more starkly than before the desperate necessity for a new race of man to surpass our own, who will stand aloof from the partisan politics of faction, and strive for his own perfection and that of his fellows. As mankind's instruments of war wax ever more bloodily sophisticated, and the nations of this Earth acquire the power to crush whole cities, perhaps whole populations, at a lightning-stroke, this need to make the human race more aptly suited to its lofty role in creation is borne ever more forcefully upon the enlightened mind.

Even now, in what will be (if time, and certain other forces, permit me indeed to complete it) my final work, I find this message directing my words, urging me to trespass once again upon the patience of my long-suffering reader. Alas, I can do it scant justice with the powers remaining to me. Suffice it to say that, while I endeavoured on this earlier occasion to expound upon my theme, the evening had drawn on, grown late and leached away into the night; and I, old man that I am, had grown intolerably weary.

At length I realised that the little fire which burned in the hearth of my study might be the occasion of this debilitating drowsiness, and I opened the french windows, letting in the night air. (My wife, who would normally admonish me against such behaviour, was away at the time visiting a sick relative.) It was chill, and my breath caught in the cold. The scent which accompanied the darkness outside, of London with its people and machines and vegetation constantly inhaling and exhaling, drew me to step out for a moment into my garden, from which I scrutinised the clear night sky.

From a young boy I have been powerfully affected by the sight of the stars. Their distance and coldness are a source of wonder to me, and I was soon wholly taken up in reverie. So sure I felt of solitude that it came as a dreadful shock when close by, as if conjured by my meditation, a young voice greeted me with a cheerful 'Hullo, Clever-clogs!'

'Good Lord!' I exclaimed, shaken but quickly realising that I was in no danger from this particular interloper. 'Whatever are you doing here, Percival?'

'Let's go inside, old man,' the figure in the darkness said at once. 'Garden fences have ears, you know.'

We retreated into my study, which was, I now acknowledged, intolerably stuffy. I left the french windows open. 'Gosh, what a fug!' Percival declared. 'Are you trying to stifle yourself, Clever-clogs, and begin our great work for us? I *was* planning on keeping you around till later on, you know.'

In the dull glow of the fire's embers, Percival looked much the same as he had been described to Emily by her perturbing policeman. (At that time Miss Blandish and I were not acquainted, and I was unaware of what had transpired that morning at St Pancras.) In my earlier book, *The Peculiar*, I have outlined Percival's appearance in these terms:

> Percival's frame is muscular yet slender, and almost simian in aspect. His ovoid head is large out of proportion to his body, like an infant's. Now in his fifteenth year, in size and development he resembles a child of perhaps ten or eleven. His eyes are large with yellowish-green irises, his pupils vesical slits like those of a cat; his ears too are large, and uniquely whorled. The back of his cranium is scrubbed with tightly curled hair, blue-black in colour, and his fingers, of which he has six on each hand, are preternaturally long and thin. His toes are also long, and unusually dexterous. His body is smooth and hairless, and his sexual characteristics underdeveloped for his age. Although his overall air attests to a sensitivity too fragile for normal human existence, Percival is in fact as strong as a mule, with that animal's hybrid vigour, and enjoys a mental resilience equal to his physical robustness.

At the time of which I am writing I had not seen Percival for five years, and yet I found him very little changed. His protracted adolescence was plainly still in progress, and a stranger might have classified the twenty-year-old as a gawky, over-intellectual lad of fourteen years or fewer.

Aware that it would vex me, Percival crossed to my writing-desk and abstracted the latest sheet of paper from my typewriter-spool. 'What are you writing now, Erik?' he asked me. (On his tongue, my familiar name takes on unwelcome overtones of patronage. I prefer my derisory nickname of 'Clever-clogs'.)

'It's just an opinion piece,' I said, annoyed at having my half-formed arguments subjected to what would undoubtedly be sharp and perceptive scrutiny.

'Oh Lord,' Percival sighed as he scanned the sheet. 'Poor old Clever-sticks. Still thinking of the future of mankind – meaning *your* kind of man, of course – when you know perfectly well he hasn't got a thing of the sort.'

'I choose to believe otherwise,' I told him coolly.

He discarded the article. 'Of course there will have to be improvements made, you're right there. And perhaps poor old *Homo sapiens* may be of use as breeding-stock. But it will be *Homo peculiar* directing the show, you know.'

The old familiar chill, such as I had not felt for half a decade, tightened across my shoulders. I moved closer to the dying fire. 'What is the matter, Percival?' I asked. 'I had thought that you were still at your Retreat. You're safer there, surely.'

His face became more sober. 'It seems some men of your kind have other ideas,' he said.

In *The Peculiar* I have recounted the events which led to Percival's foundation of the Retreat, in the late years of the recent war. Since that volume is now difficult to come by, I suppose that here I had better give a brief account of those matters, and of Percival's early life.

3. THE STORY OF PERCIVAL

He had been an infant prodigy, of course. Intellectually capable beyond his years, he was uncannily sensitive to the moods and thoughts of others. He was a voracious reader in every subject from the age of sixteen months, and had devoured first children's and then adult reading matter, throwing himself with equal zeal into practical studies as diverse as engineering, veterinary science (for he grew up on a farm) and musical performance.

He had put his mother, a highly intelligent woman of German parentage, through a long and difficult confinement: she had died a few days after his birth, leaving Percival in the care of his father and aunt. Theirs was a modestly well-to-do Cornish family, whose ancient Celtic stock had been infused, perhaps since pre-Roman times, with the blood of successive exotic visitors to Cornwall's shores. Percival's father, who had been a child at the time of the Great War, joined up soon after the more recent hostilities were declared, and died in France when Percival was twelve.

By then, the boy had for some time been running the large farm between his studies, and had, over the course of two generations of animals, improved the livestock's milk and egg yields fourfold. He had trained the family sheepdogs to perform complicated manoeuvres, suggestive of an unprecedented rapport between beast and master, and had designed a number of automated techniques for husbanding the stock which had allowed the farm to function with remarkable efficiency during the wartime absence of many of the labourers. After her brother's death Percival's aunt besought Dr Tremaine, the local medical practitioner and a close neighbour who had known and treated her nephew since birth, for help with the boy's ever more stringent demands for education. Tremaine was an old friend of mine, and when I heard of the young phenomenon I rashly volunteered to undertake this task.

Percival left the family farm and came to live in London with my wife and me. Very soon, his mental acuity had put to shame not only my own talents, but those of a number of quite prominent scholars, scientists and writers of my acquaintance, whom I shall not embarrass once again by naming here. The boy rapidly outstripped my best attempts at instruction, and proceeded to direct his own studies, and indeed his own career, along lines of his own choosing. However, his tender age meant that he still had use for an adult who could act for him in certain matters, and he remained habitually resident at my house when his investigations did not carry him elsewhere.

The young genius became fond of me in his own aloof way, and it was in me that he confided when his biological researches, now advanced beyond my ability to follow, delivered him to a startling conclusion. He was (he explained to me blithely) one of a handful in his generation who were forerunners of an entirely new species of man, which he fancifully dubbed *Homo peculiar*. He was convinced that, a few generations from now, men and women like himself would be the dominant creatures on the planet, while men like me might expect to be at best their servants or domestic pets. At worst, we would be extinct: our world's new masters might well decide that our selfishly jealous tendencies constituted a threat to them, and eliminate its source.

I had needed some convincing on these points, to say the least of it, but Percival was a compelling advocate. His unique appearance had worked in his favour, and at length I had conceded (it was not in fact difficult to believe) that the boy was of a biological type quite apart from his family and peers, myself included. He was, not inhuman, but human in a different, more developed mode than that of normal men.

As Percival had entered his prolonged pubertal period, he had begun to make contact, by means of mental disciplines which allowed him to 'tune in' to their psychic vibrations, with other 'supernormal' adolescents. It was with some of these, when finally they came into physical proximity with one another, that he began the social and sexual experiments which characterised this phase of his life, and which so scandalised our conventional neighbours.

In this behaviour, I am afraid that Percival miscalculated badly. He had underestimated the tendency of *Homo sapiens* to fear that which he cannot understand, and to punish those who offend against his sense of normality. It was not very long afterward that Percival was accused of being in league with England's enemies: he was, after all, of partial German stock, no matter that his father had fought valiantly against the Germans and been killed by them. By now Percival had many friends in the scientific establishment, and it had come to be suspected that the young outsider was abusing their good nature in order to spy upon top-secret matters relating to the war effort.

The very idea was ludicrous, of course. It was an article of faith with Percival (which I confess that I had never discouraged) that his kind was above national affinities. He was no more likely to give aid to a foreign power than to his native land. It seems now that there were some who hoped to use these accusations as an inducement to set Percival's considerable talents to working for the Allied cause, but this was always a vain hope. An arrest for espionage was followed by an ingenious yet appallingly dangerous escape on Percival's part, and a desperate period which he spent in constant evasion of the police. At length the young man was left with no alternative but to withdraw, along with his peculiar companions, to that remote location which they called the Retreat.

I had offered to accompany them, but they were in no state of mind to welcome the society of normal men. Since then I had received a total of two communications from Percival, from which I understood that he and and his comrades had progressed in their various endeavours, including their attempts to reach out telepathically to others of their kind across the world. These efforts had succeeded in gathering together at the Retreat a band of supernormal children and adolescents from far afield: additionally, they had fostered the founding of 'communities of the peculiar' in other continents, with whom they were in constant psychic communion. Now, it seemed, this fragile international rapport was under dire threat.

4. THE INTRUDER AT THE WINDOW

'They haven't found the Retreat yet,' Percival told me, warming his hands at my dying fire. 'There's that, at least. But it's a rotten situation, Erik. We lost contact with Maurita's group in Argentina months ago now, and our friends in Russia are on the run. They're confused and panicking – we can't get any sense out of them. The New Zealand commune was always too far away to get a clear signal – the Earth gets in the way, you know – but now Nombeko's people in South Africa can't contact them either.'

I asked, 'But who is it that's doing this, Percival?'

He shrugged. 'Some kind of soldier gang. They're well armed and well trained, and they seem to have a rudimentary grasp of strategy and tactics. Who they're working for, we don't know – one of your silly countries or another, I suppose. We think they must have been picking off the lonely ones, the supernormals who won't join our communities, for years now. We simply didn't notice. Now they've started on our nerve-centres.'

I was horrified, of course, at the idea of Percival's friends, children as they were, being hunted or persecuted. If I am to be unreservedly honest, however, I felt at the idea of these arrogant supermen being cut down to size a palpably vindictive thrill. It was years since I had been in regular communication with Percival, and the calm certainty with which he habitually imbued his outrageous assertions had had little opportunity to work on me of late. I told myself that it would be perverse to hope that the brutal and ignorant might prevail at the expense of the wise and enlightened. Of course the highest type, morally and spiritually as well as intellectually, should triumph: such is the way of nature, and it is gloriously right that it should be so. Sternly then I quelled my rebellious, unworthy glee and asked, 'What can I do?'

Percival laughed shortly, then cocked his head a little, as if suddenly distracted. 'There's not a lot that *you* can do, dear Clever-clogs. A couple of us are in town, that's all, finding out what we can from some people we know, and I thought I'd look you up while we were here and tell you the news. This is awfully awkward, I don't mind telling you. We may have to bring forward our plans for the terminal –'. Quite suddenly he broke off speaking and sprang across the room, out of the glass doors and into the night, disorientating me completely. At that moment he seemed more like a frog than a monkey, and more like either than a man. From outside came a bellow of alarm followed by a violent scuffling.

'Good heavens!' I inadequately exclaimed. I have never been a fighter. Even in the Great War, I performed volunteer work as a medical orderly: I saw considerable action, but had no hand in combat. Even if I had, that would have been over thirty years ago, and I could scarcely expect my failing body to sustain such work now. Nevertheless (and shockingly capable though I knew Percival to be when necessary), I could not allow him to face alone what might be an armed man, or body of men. Grasping the poker, I stepped out nervously into the garden, where a pair of indistinct shapes was writhing in savage union. Percival's spidery limbs were wrapped about the intruder, whose leather coat flapped and slapped fishlike against the flagstone path. The two of them resembled a pair of symbiotic organisms, united in some violent otherworldly coupling.

Such fancies come upon me often, at the most inopportune moments. As I stood gathering my courage, the larger man turned his head towards me. In the dim light from the study door, I saw to my surprise that he was a Negro, with a fine-boned face, neat goatee beard and expressive eyes. Mystifyingly, he appeared to react to the sight of me with quite as much astonishment. So surprised was he, in fact, that Percival was able with a moment's struggle to pin him to the ground and straddle his chest, his limber hands pressing the man's wrists into the earth.

Still amazed by whatever it was that he perceived in my countenance, the Negro swore. From the intonation, and his choice of oath, I could tell that he was an American. 'Help me out, Erik!' Percival exclaimed, turning to face me. He frowned, then his expression altered uncharacteristically into what, on someone else's visage, I would have taken for confusion or even fear. 'Erik?' he said, with unusual diffidence. 'Who's that behind your face?'

Fearing a third intrusion, I span around in alarm and looked about the study. No-one was present, although a log fell in the fireplace, disturbed by a sudden breeze. I turned back to ask Percival what he had meant, but there was no-one there. He and the American had vanished silently, from barely five feet in front of me.

For a long while, I gave serious thought to what I ought to do. Percival had said enough to give me grave misgivings for his safety; yet I had the strong impression that, wherever he and the Negro had disappeared to, it was nowhere I might follow them. Nor did I have any idea of where to seek the companion with whom Percival was visiting town, and after a moment's consideration I realised that this person (whom I probably would not know) would very likely be in hiding in any case.

At length, and with a somewhat familiar sense that Percival's affairs were frustratingly beyond my scope to help or hinder, I decided that there was no action I could take. I waited, in the hope that one or both men might return as abruptly as they had left, but nothing of the kind occurred. After a short while I fetched my pipe from my desk drawer, lit it with an ember and smoked quietly, once again contemplating the night sky.

Quite recently, or so it seemed to me, the stars over London had been hatched across by searchlight beams and streaks of fire, traversed by men encased in flimsy machinery and bound on errands of desperate hostility. Since then, peace had prevailed; and yet man even now might be preparing for a crisis still more troubling, one from whose effects he, and perhaps the world that gave him birth, might never recover.

Still though, those sparks of cosmic fire blazed down indifferent, and this came as a welcome comfort to me.

II: DIVERSE ENCOUNTERS

1. ENTER MR SPEARS

On the following day I received two further visits, neither of them so dramatic as the encroachments of the previous evening, but each with its own significant consequences.

The first of these appointments had been arranged for some time. My caller was St John Spears, a wealthy American philanthropist with whom I had been in correspondence. The interest he had taken in my writings, both novelistic and philosophical, had been flattering, an occurrence which (I ruefully considered) had been altogether too uncommon in recent years. Mr Spears arrived in the middle of the morning, driven by a chauffeur whom I awkwardly invited to wait out the meeting in my sitting-room, while I entertained his employer in the study.

Mr Spears bore little resemblance to my visitors of the preceding night. He was a dynamic figure of perhaps half my age, with a high forehead, a wide, almost lipless mouth and narrow eyes, and compensated for his relatively small stature by remaining in constant, forceful motion. He politely refused my offer of a seat, and took a glass of neat soda-water in place of the whisky which I poured myself. As we spoke he stood restlessly, sporadically forgetting himself and pacing a few steps in one direction or another, before recollecting his manners. From his appearance I guessed that he must have both Jew and Spaniard in his ancestry, and certainly he exhibited that mongrel vitality which so distinguishes the white American from his staid European cousin.

I had hopes of encouraging my guest to take an interest in some plans which I had drawn up years before: a programme of social and biological improvement which would require the support of a weighty coalition of political and private backers if it were ever to receive tangible application. The project involved, at a mundane level, the promotion of matrimony between individuals selected from the population as having desirable heritable characteristics; the encouragement of voluntary sterilisation among those less favoured by nature; and certain experiments in breeding from contrasting varieties of the species, as for instance the Ethiopian with the Eskimo, or the Maori with the Masai, in an effort to identify those which produced the strongest and most vital strains.

'As you no doubt remember,' I told my visitor now, 'between the wars schemes such as this one enjoyed great popularity among the educated classes in both our continents. Sadly there has been a falling-off of interest in recent years. The war has, I fear, intervened to sap men's idealism, turning them against the kind of social engineering which our race so desperately needs.'

In fact I had long since despaired of ever finding backing for the venture. I had assumed, foolishly perhaps, that as an ardent reader of my work Mr Spears would make at least a sympathetic listener; and so he was (although as I have indicated he brought to our encounter a restlessness which I found disconcerting), but little more. He spoke perceptively of incidents in recent history and of the developments which, in their light, the immediate future might be expected to bring; and he professed a profound interest in the question of interplanetary travel and colonisation, another of my perennials and one on which I had addressed the British Rocket Group some years before. (Mr Spears claimed to have been in the audience on that occasion, although I had no memory of him.) Most unusually for one of his nationality, and all the more so for a prosperous man, he spoke approvingly of international socialism as an ideal, although he admitted to reservations about its practice.

I may be an old man, and naturally vain as I dare say many authors are, but I have not yet succumbed to geriatric imbecility. It would have been quite clear that Spears was flattering me, and that his visit had an ulterior purpose, even had I not had cause to be wary (and of his countrymen in particular) following the occurrences of the evening before. So it transpired: once he reckoned that he had humoured me for long enough to put me at my ease, Spears turned the conversation around to the subject of my novels, and of *The Peculiar* in particular.

'It's a funny thing,' Spears mused, glancing sideways at me as he brought himself up short from a brief bout of pacing. 'That book was published as fiction, one of your English "scientific romances", like Mr Wells'. That was the line all your reviewers took anyway, the ones who read it. But I think there's more to it than that. You start off saying, "This is a true tale: while the names of the participants have been altered," or something, "I myself witnessed many of the events recounted herein, while others were divulged to me afterward by unimpeachable witnesses." Forgive me if I'm not word-perfect –' (he was not) '– but it looks to me like your book wants to have the cake and eat it. So which is it, Mr Clevedon? Is *The Peculiar* a made-up story, or a real one?'

I took a deep breath, smiled and said, 'It's a traditional pretence in fiction, Mr Spears. The author must pretend that the things which he has imagined are all true, and his readers must pretend that they believe him. I am scarcely the first novelist who has affected to have witnessed events with his own eyes, nor will I be the last.'

'Right,' Spears said impatiently. 'But, Mr Clevedon, a lot of what you tell in that book really did happen. Your military intelligence services *did* arrest a fifteen-year-old boy for espionage towards the end of the war, and he really did escape, in a way which looks a lot like what you put in your book. His name was –' and he gave Percival's real name, the one which I have not used either here or elsewhere.

I nodded. 'I recall the case,' I said. 'It was in large part what inspired me to write the tale I did. Young _____ must have been a strangely gifted child, and the strangely gifted have always been an interest of mine.'

'I'm interested in gifted children too,' said Spears. He raised his hands, in a typically expansive gesture of submission, and continued:

'OK, I'll lay my cards on the table. It's my belief that these kids of yours are real, and I want to help them. That's why I'm here. Like yourself I take an interest in the future of mankind, and it sounds to me like those children could *be* that future. From what you wrote in your story I guess you think so too.'

'The novel's narrator certainly thinks so, Mr Spears. But I'm afraid he was as fictional as Percival and Bridget and the other characters. He has some qualities in common with me, just as Percival is partially based on what I could find out about young _____, but he has no more real an existence than they. I'm very sorry to have wasted your time.'

'Hear me out,' Spears said doggedly. 'At the end of your book, you have "Percival" and his pals going off to start a new life for themselves on an island in the South Seas. Now, they're gifted kids as we've said, with a lot of ingenuity and practical sense. But an island can't provide the resources they need to build a proper civilised society. It's no life for a child, Mr Clevedon, living like a savage. I'm a rich man as you know, a very rich man. I can get hold of engineers, building materials, fertilisers, agriculturalists ...'

He paused then. I suppose that, if I had come to the conversation unforewarned, I might have blurted out at that point that Percival (that was to say my character) had been an expert in agriculture, and thus confirmed Spears' conjecture that to me that young man's existence was no mere fiction. It seemed as if the characteristic crudeness of the American's approach might still mask certain subtleties.

Fortunately, the previous night I had been forewarned by Percival himself. 'I am very sorry,' I told Mr Spears, with all the sincerity I could muster. 'I don't know what else I may say to convince you. If my characters truly existed, I am sure that they would be most grateful to find themselves added to your roster of good causes. However, you will understand that, as they *are* my characters, such a thing would be categorically impossible. I am sorry if anything I wrote has caused you to make such an unfortunate error.'

Spears sighed sharply. The noise recalled vividly to me my time in France, and the cough of a Stokes' mortar exhaling its lethal charge. I was alone in my house, and Percival had said that the 'soldier gang' which was pursuing him and his associates was ruthless. If St John Spears were one of its number, then it might well occur to him to threaten me for information. Even in my prime I had entertained no illusions as to my own capacity for heroism under torture.

To my intense relief, however, Spears merely thanked me curtly, and stood up to leave.

An hour later, after I had retired to my sitting-room and consumed a second whisky and soda (which I felt I had singularly merited), I heard a low whispering in the study, and a quiet voice called out, 'Erik?'

'Percival?' I replied, greatly relieved. 'Is that you?' Instead of my youthful friend, however, two women entered, having evidently let themselves in through the french windows which I had believed were locked.

It was my first meeting with Emily Blandish, and for that matter with Violet, although I recognised immediately that the latter bore a selection of those physiognomic and anatomical oddities which distinguish Percival's kind from the mass of 'normal' humanity. Emily I found to be a strikingly attractive, thoughtful woman in whose level gaze I discerned a strange admixture of worldliness and nervous innocence. She was one who had seen a great deal of what men have made of the world, and yet retained a cautious optimism regarding its future. I warmed to her.

'Percival said to come here if there was trouble,' the younger woman said without preamble. 'There's a bloke watching the street, though, so we came in the back.' Her voice was confident and clear, her accent pure East London.

2. VIOLET AND THE CONSTABLES

Violet was seventeen years old, and had been recruited to the Retreat after Percival and the others had made telepathic contact with her some three years since. She had had a rough childhood, in which her natural aptitude for thievery had been severely tested. Certainly born illegitimate, and very likely the product of incest, her unusual appearance had made her repulsive even to those of her immediate family. For her as for many others, the Retreat had been a welcome sanctuary. Her familiarity with certain of London's less exemplary neighbourhoods and communities had been what had made Percival choose her as his companion on his return to the city.

Between them, Emily and Violet acquainted me with the episode leading to the latter's arrest at St Pancras, and with what had occurred thereafter. The girl had been taken by the sinister policemen, who she was quite convinced were not policemen, to an ordinary-looking town-house which was most certainly not a police station, and incarcerated in a cell. This room appeared to have been recently adapted to its current purpose. A sturdy metal plate had been let into the wall, and to this Violet was handcuffed.

Having made sure of Violet's immobility, the 'policemen' exchanged their uniforms for functional boiler-suits, retaining the electronic headpieces which Emily had observed beneath their helmets. As Emily had realised at the railway station, Violet's peculiar talents included a kind of hypnotic suggestion at a distance, akin but not identical to Percival's telepathy. By playing on the suggestibility of the human mind, Violet was capable of persuading an observer not to notice her, thus rendering herself effectively invisible even when committing a public crime. She had been able to exert this power evenly across a large and ever-changing crowd; and it had been sporadically effective even upon Emily, who had considerable experience of mental influences and who besides had had her attention by then fully focused on her quarry. If this same gift had failed to affect the false policemen, then these aural contrivances (which Violet now speculated acted as an artificial aid to concentration) were undoubtedly responsible.

The treatment which Violet had received in the town-house had been very brutal, although it was clear to her that the men had been instructed not to kill or maim her. She harboured no illusions, however, that this arrangement would persist indefinitely. Her captors had been seeking information about the location of the Retreat, and secondarily about the current whereabouts of Percival, whom they knew by name. Violet was contemptuous of their efforts to persuade her to talk: a mind like hers, she said, was hardly going to give its friends away out of sheer terror, merely because some human animals were making sure her body hurt.

Whether she would have remained so sanguine after a longer time in captivity, I cannot tell. In any case, Violet set about arranging an escape at her earliest convenience. Her first act once left alone was to attempt to communicate telepathically with Percival, but she found that young man beset by difficulties of his own. (This had been the afternoon before his nocturnal visit to my house, and I would soon learn that he and that night's other intruder had had an earlier encounter around this time.) She turned instead to the group-mind of the supernormals at the Retreat, which was large enough and diffuse enough to communicate in the aggregate even at so distant a remove.

The supernormals' understanding of their own capabilities had developed enormously since that time when Percival had carried out his own risky abscondment from military custody. Working as a single entity, with Violet's mind as its focal point, the community was able to locate in the vicinity of the house a middle-aged priest, formerly an army chaplain, who while most certainly not a member of the higher species had a degree of mental sensitivity considerably more developed than the norm. This was sufficiently acute to render him susceptible to suggestion by the group-mind, and that night the unfortunate man dreamed feverishly of confinement, of being trapped, cut off from all his fellows and his world.

He awoke with the confused but overwhelming notion that there was a soul in need of his immediate and specific aid. In something of a trance state, he located his service revolver, walked to the house where Violet was being held prisoner, and broke in through a rear window. He shot two of the guards as they tried to defend the building, wounding one in the thigh and killing the other outright, then released Violet from her bondage shortly before the wounded man succeeded in summoning aid. Violet fled, leaving her deliverer to the mercies of her erstwhile captors.

Although I should have been expecting something of the kind, both Emily and I were appalled by Violet's callousness toward her rescuer. Violet was quite sanguine about the man's sacrifice, however. His involvement had been necessary, not merely expedient, and the exchange of his life for her freedom had been a simple matter of priority. I was familiar with this cold-hearted type of moral calculation from my conversations with Percival, and I knew that it was what made such actions as Violet's thievery, essential as it was to finance her and Percival's investigations among London's underworld, acceptable to them both.

'He was a superstitious, silly man anyway,' Violet said contemptuously, her errant cockney vowels and elusive consonants suddenly recalling Percival's more educated tones. 'Maybe he *was* brighter than the average for one of you, but he didn't understand the things his half-open mind let him see. He caught the fringes of the thought-talk of his betters, and thought he heard the voices of angels, or messages from God. He never could have been one of us, even if the church hadn't got to him so young as it did.' She refused all further discussion on the matter, saying, 'Of course you can't understand,' as if that was an end to it.

After her release, Violet had delayed in following Percival's instructions that they should rendezvous, if separated, at my house. Considering that, in comparison with the fraudulent policemen, Emily was very much the lesser of two evils, she had returned quite coolly to the railway station, apparently expecting to find her former pursuer looking for her there; as, indeed, she was.

By this time Emily was concerned that she had received no word from her own associate, the man who had fought with Percival in my garden on the previous night. (I was relieved to learn that, despite their common nationality, the interloper had had no connection with St John Spears: like Violet, I could not believe that Emily was involved with the 'soldier gang', and the latter was willing to vouch without reservation for her Negro friend.) After her initial encounter with Violet, Emily had left St Pancras station with the firm conviction that the peculiar pickpocket was someone of importance to their work. Having exhausted all her other avenues of enquiry, she had returned to the station in hopes of discovering where the policemen might have taken their young prisoner.

The two women had met at the railway station. It seemed that, during their transient encounter, Emily had made as enduring an impression on the young thief as the latter on her. To me it looked as if Violet had decided arbitrarily to take Emily into her confidence as Percival had once taken me; regarding her as part adult protector, part agent among mundane human society, and perhaps (I did not flatter myself, and so I should not flatter Emily) part pet.

All this I learned from Emily and Violet. For my part I gave an account of my dialogue with Spears, who Violet considered was very likely in collusion with her persecutors. 'He wanted the location of the Retreat,' I confirmed, 'just like your policemen. At present, he still thinks it's in the South Seas.'

'Percival said you never should have written that bloody book,' said Violet calmly. 'It's too late now, though.' Her most pressing concern was that she could no longer make contact with Percival. 'I can't get hold of him,' she complained, as if irked by a faulty telephone connection. 'He's usually there – all of them are – in the background of my thoughts. It's like – well, *you'll* understand it best if I say it's like a roomful of people, all talking at once. If you listen out carefully, you can hear one particular voice, even if you can't make out just what it's saying, you know? Since last night I can't "hear" Percival, however hard I try. Nor can the others.'

'He isn't dead,' I reassured her. 'At least, I don't believe so. He may have ... gone ... somewhere else, though.' I explained, as best I could, the scene which I had witnessed the previous night, after the struggle between Percival and the black man. 'I had wondered if this was a new ability Percival had developed – to move from one place to another instantaneously, *in extremis*. There are accounts of saints and mystics performing similar feats ... but I suppose, if you don't recognise the phenomenon, it mustn't have been.'

'I think I know what must have happened,' Emily said. 'Certainly, if Percival's as unusual as you say, it has to be a possibility.' She went on to explain something of the astounding talent of her friend, my second unexpected visitor of the previous night. It is of this man, and of his remarkable qualities, that I must now tell.

3. THE STORY OF LECHASSEUR

Honoré Lechasseur was by birth a New Orleanian, fetched up in London by that indefatigable tide of men and munitions which broke against the western shores of Europe in the later stages of the war. When afterward I had the opportunity to question him, he proved strangely reticent on the subject, but I have no doubt that, of his race, his family must have been a remarkable one. Very likely, as with so many inhabitants of that colourful city, his ancestors' African strain had become partially mixed with those of the European and American Indian. What is certain is that, although he displayed both that physical toughness and that lassitude which commingle so paradoxically yet so uncompromisingly in the character of the American Negro, he was in other respects atypical of the type, possessing both an astute intellect and a much heightened sensitivity to the minutest details of his surroundings.

Lechasseur had had, as people say, 'a bad war'. During a tour of duty in France and Belgium a violent explosion, of which he was the only survivor from his platoon, threatened to cripple him, and for a long time his doctors were adamant that he would never recover the power of walking. The psychic trauma which he suffered was quite as severe, and Lechasseur spent a period of several years in a state of sullen despondency, troubled by strange and savage dreams. At length the use of his limbs returned to him, and with it an altogether rarer faculty, one which he now believes had been lying latent within him since his boyhood.

To his gradual astonishment, Lechasseur found that he was sometimes able to *perceive time*: not merely the passage of it, but the shapes and patterns that it makes in present, past and future. At first such perceptions took the form of shapeless premonitions and forebodings, or memories of places and events at which he had not himself been present. By stages it became apparent to him that these visions were related to the persons with whom, or more rarely the objects with which, he came into contact. Sometimes they acquired a startling clarity, in which Lechasseur seemed to see the individual before him as a cross-section of a larger being, consisting of that man in his chronological entirety, the sum of all that he had been and would be across the span of his life. These 'flesh-worms' were a disturbing 'sight' (for, although the perceptual process involved was certainly not vision in its strictest sense, sight remained for Lechasseur the closest available analogy), tapering as they did towards twin tails at birth and death.

(Occasionally he would encounter stranger manifestations still. When first he glimpsed Percival, Lechasseur perceived what he called 'red threads' woven throughout the young man's body, stretching away from him through days and years toward a very distant future. It was as if the supernormal youth had been a puppet stitched from cloth, but one whose controlling strings were those very seams which held its body together. But here I anticipate myself.)

Shortly after Emily and Lechasseur first made one another's acquaintance, they discovered that Emily had an equally exceptional gift, one which was complementary to Lechasseur's own and which could take effect only within the context of it. For whereas Lechasseur was sensitive to time, Emily was able incredibly to *move about within it*, stepping out along the line of someone else's life and following their 'time-line' like a spoor. For this she was required to be in physical contact with Lechasseur, or someone like him: without his special senses she would have been travelling blind, and would likely have vanished never to return.

Over the course of their association, the diverse pair had come to realise that these abilities on which they could call, while rare, were not unique. A small proportion of the human race fell into one or another (yet seemingly never both) of these categories of 'time-sensitive' and 'time-channeller'. (It was evident to me, when I was told of this, that such abilities were not themselves indications of 'peculiar' status: rather, they were a rare but natural talent both of *Homo peculiar* and of *Homo sapiens*, which had remained latent until recent generations.)

Most such individuals, never coming into contact with a member of the complementary type, remained ignorant of their extraordinary faculty. When I related to Emily the events which I had witnessed, or rather which I had failed to witness, through my french windows that night, it was her immediate supposition that Percival was a time-channeller in addition to his other attributes. It seemed that my momentary queer perception of him and Lechasseur as a symbiotic double-entity had had an element of truth about it.

This much Violet and I learned from Emily, that afternoon. To address the sequel to that scene, in what time and what place it was that Lechasseur and Percival found themselves, after the latter had unwittingly pitched them away through time from that June evening of 1950, and whose personal path through history it was that they followed on that journey, I must turn to the account of Lechasseur himself, as he related it to me some time later.

In the telephone call which she had made to him from her home, Emily had conveyed to Lechasseur both the general area in which she had seen Violet, and the description both of the young woman and of her accomplice, which she had received from the supposed PC Grayles. Given these individuals' unusual appearances, it had been for Lechasseur a matter of a few hours' work to discover the building in which they had been staying. Since his recovery he had made for himself a somewhat dubious living by working as a combination of black-market trader and private detective, and consequently he was a man of many contacts, placed both high and low among the assorted citizenry of the capital.

The premises in question, whose precise location is immaterial for our purposes, were the surviving half of a partly collapsed terrace of houses which had been bombed during the war, and which had as yet been neither rebuilt nor demolished. Many such remain in London, and they tend to attract those who have reason, good or (more usually) bad, to avoid the city's more reputable sources of accommodation.

Lechasseur had this fact clearly in mind as he bicycled towards this address, and upon his arrival at the half-fallen row of houses he essayed a cautious approach. Emily had warned him that the young man whom he was to find might have abilities beyond the ordinary, and after the veritable bestiary of such talents which their work together had uncovered Lechasseur had no inclination to be sceptical. Although such a thing would have been contrary to his usual habit, he wondered as he approached the building whether he ought not to have brought with him a gun, and this image was to the forefront of his mind, together with a clear mental picture of the person he was seeking, as he entered the building. To Percival, with his acute telepathic awareness and his worry that he and his friends were presently being sought by armed men, Lechasseur's approach could scarcely have been more obvious.

Finding each of the terrace's front doors boarded across, Lechasseur gained entry by climbing through the frame of a long-absent window. He found the interior of the house heaped with rubble, which a succession of the transitory inhabitants had made attempts to clear, with partial success. He shouted, 'Hey! Is anyone at home?', but was rebuffed by silence. His nervous agitation brought with it an uncannily precise sense of his surroundings, which in turn pricked at his temporal perceptions. These latter stirred and awakened as he began to climb the steps towards the upper storey of the first house of the terrace: shadows compromised the clarity of his vision, and ghosts of furniture and decorations long since rotten dogged his senses. Huddled heaps of mortar and masonry appeared to stir and get to their feet, only to fall back when he turned his direct gaze upon them.

Upstairs Lechasseur found that a hole had been knocked through into the next-door house, using some heavy implement such as a sledgehammer. He climbed across into the next property before confirming that this upper room was also empty. Echoes of past and future inhabitants flickered across his sensibility, and he screwed his eyelids close together in a vain attempt to filter out this onslaught of lost time. In this way he proceeded, checking first the ground floor and then the upper storey of each house, while images streamed past him of the families and individuals who once had lived there. Before his eyes children grew older and left home, while their grandparents regressed from dotage into youthful vigour.

Presently Lechasseur came to a stairway which had crumpled into beams and splinters, leaving a precarious banister which he gingerly scaled to reach the upper-storey landing. As in each of the houses, a bedroom adjoined it, and this he checked for signs of life. For a moment as he entered he caught sight of Percival crouched in the far corner, and in that instant gained his strange impression that the young man's body was shot through with red threads of futurity. Then, in an instant, he was confounded by a premonition of what that place will be, decades from now: a dark, low-ceilinged space delirious with noise and flashing light, where young people, half-nude, writhed and gyrated in an arrhythmic frenzy. Pounding, outlandish music pressed against his ears, and pyrotechnic colours flashed at him from all directions.

Confused and disorientated, Lechasseur cried out and fell to his knees. As the oppressive vision span away from him, he saw again the dim and dingy room, and the lithe and ape-like figure of Percival leaping at him, arms outstretched. As the boy barrelled into him Lechasseur shouted, 'I'm not here to hurt you! I just want to talk!', and then, toppled by his attacker's momentum, he tumbled down the erstwhile stairwell into the debris below. For several moments he believed the building was falling along with him, masonry crashing down about his shoulders and chest. Whether this was a memory of the bomb's arrival several years before, or a premonition of the terrace's eventual demolition, he could not tell. Then Percival was upon him once more, belabouring him about the face and arms.

Feebly Lechasseur tried to ward off his assailant's blows, before finding his confusion abruptly intensified a thousandfold, as in his mind's eye centuries of past and future fires and plagues, wars and disasters ravaged that minute portion of London. One moment he felt himself underwater in some forgotten inundation; then above him, clearly somehow through the house's roof, he saw a vast circular vessel spinning through the sky like a leisurely top, its hatches pouring fire onto the streets below. Then awareness itself vanished, and Lechasseur succumbed to a darkness which was beset by evil dreams.

4. THE PURSUIT OF PERCIVAL

At length he was awakened by one of the building's other temporary occupants. The elderly female vagrant objected to his presence, and made her complaints known with a hail of blows which sufficed to recall the black man to the here and now. Aching and dazed, but realising at once that this poor frightened creature deserved no harm from him, Lechasseur made an embarrassed apology and left, emerging into the early evening of a London street and to the realisation that his bicycle was missing.

Exhausted, sore, frustrated and angry, Lechasseur sat down on a crumbling wall and pondered his position. It was now obvious to him that the hypersensitivity which his extra-temporal percipience had suffered inside the building had been effected by none other than Percival himself, in what can only be described as a form of telepathic attack. Lechasseur's visions had increased in intensity as he approached the room which held the boy, and they had swiftly swelled to overcome him once he was in the young man's presence. Emily had been perfectly correct to suggest that he might find their quarry in possession of some special defences. (It did not occur to Lechasseur at this point that Percival might have been a time-channeller. Indeed I believe that the specific mode of this assault was accidental, the unhappy result of Percival's instinctively identifying a 'weak spot' in Lechasseur's psychic defences.)

The Negro shortly came to realise, however, that the boy's attack had had one lingering and probably unlooked-for side-effect. An echo of the enhanced sensitivity imposed upon his time-senses still remained, like a fading of the sky following the sunset, and as it proved would endure for several hours more before it finally quiesced. To his inner eye a faint but distinct form was visible in front of the house, a long shadow not itself a flesh-worm so much as a worm-cast or a snake's sloughed skin, stretching from the spot where Lechasseur had left his bicycle to the nearest street-corner, where it vanished from view behind a row of intact houses.

Lechasseur realised that, if he was to recover his property, he would be in for a very long walk. Painfully he stood, and began following in the vehicle's wake and that of its rider.

Over the course of the next five or six hours, Lechasseur trailed Percival to a variety of locations, in each of which the latter had apparently conducted a hasty search for Violet. One of these places was St Pancras, where as far as the Negro could ascertain from the lad's fading traces, he had caught one glimpse of the policeman on duty and fled.

It was near midnight by the time that Lechasseur eventually reached the rear garden of my house, by which time all but the faintest glimmer of Percival's passage had vanished from his waning perceptions. He found his bicycle where Percival had discarded it in a flower-bed, near the patch of light cast on the lawn from my french windows. Fatigued though he was, the black man understood that he would have to be alert and well-prepared if he was to face Percival again. Silently, as far as possible, he manoeuvred himself into a position whence he might spy upon my study's warm and welcoming interior. It was, as things would turn out, the last glimpse of familiarity he would be granted for some time.

At once, Percival emerged from the house like a Dervish, colliding with him, pummelling and pounding, and followed (at a distance and diffidently, as you will recall) by myself. As he was grappled to the ground, Lechasseur felt the probing of the young man's mind at the borders of his own; this time, however, he was able to turn it aside. Despite this, his awareness of the shapes of time began to open like a flower, and once again those bloody strands of future life were visible, pulling this way and that at Percival's body and limbs. It was at this point that Lechasseur glimpsed me standing in the doorway, and was so startled by what he perceived that Percival was able to gain his momentary advantage.

It was Lechasseur's perception (and you must believe me when I tell you that, had I been made aware then of the apparition, I would have been at an absolute loss to account for it) that my face was not my face: rather, it seemed a wax mask, flimsy and hollow, behind which an entirely *other* face observed the two men's struggle. You must remember that this semblance presented itself to Lechasseur's time-senses, not to his ocular vision; still, that visage 'appeared' to him warped and bestial, and it was staring, with an icy detachment blending in equal parts amusement and contempt, directly at Percival and himself.

When presently he had successfully pinioned Lechasseur's arms against the ground, Percival also turned to face me. Whether as a result of his bodily contact with the Negro, which as I have learned facilitates the interplay of the time-channelling and time-sensitive faculties, or thanks to that tenuous mental connection he had succeeded in establishing between them, he saw me, his friend, for a moment through Lechasseur's eyes. At once he asked, 'Who's that behind your face?' The astonishment which at that moment was shared by the two men, the focus of their joint attention on those hideous features lurking behind my own, abruptly flung them into the abyss of time, along the trajectory which that mystifying question had defined.

As Lechasseur would tell me later, sounding somewhat aggrieved, 'The travelling doesn't usually take *time*. What time is there for it to happen in? The farthest Emily and I had been before was something like a hundred and fifty years. That seemed like nothing – one blink, then we were there, like falling asleep in one place and waking up some place else. That's not how it felt this time round.' Their course being apparently pre-determined, it felt to Lechasseur as if he and Percival were falling, unable to direct their flight, clinging together now not out of antagonism but in the sheer need for human contact in the crackling electric void through which it seemed they hurtled. After a long duration, as it felt to Lechasseur, they found themselves beached against solidity, and fell apart to lie gasping on pitiless ground.

It was long minutes before Lechasseur was capable of opening his eyes, and of beholding above his head a sky of blurry stars. Each glowed with a bluish cast whose unfamiliarity chilled him to the bone. His temporal perceptions, overloaded perhaps, were silent. He tried to raise his head, but the muscles of his neck seemed enervated, and he fell back painfully. It felt as if his body lay upon a bed of nails or needles, which bore him up sturdily through his leather coat but mercilessly pricked at his head and hands. The air was thick and moist, and uncomfortably warm. Mustering all the strength he could, Lechasseur lifted his head once more, and saw that, as he later put it, 'Nothing around me made the slightest sense.'

He lay beside Percival on what appeared to be a grassy plain, beneath a sky whose uniform tint was that of late evening, and whose smeared stars were shepherded by a far brighter, whiter point of light. No moon was visible, and no sun either. A cliff, so gigantic that he could not tell whether it were near or distant, rose smooth and darkly purple, obscuring a large portion of the sky. The 'grass' around him was bright yellow in colour, and it was not grass. Each stalk was a stiff, flattened thorn, long and sharp as a knife. Lechasseur's head swam, and against his will it fell back onto blades which stabbed his scalp like poignards.

'Percival,' a voice, or what sounded as if it might have been a voice, said from behind him. Lechasseur stared into the sky as sounds like heavy footfalls made their approach. Incredibly, his peculiar companion had succeeded in clambering to his feet. The youth stood hunched, as if his frame bore a great weight, but his demeanour was assured.

'I saw you,' he said, addressing the approaching presence. 'You live behind Erik's face. I … I suppose I must have followed you here.' His voice held puzzlement, but also pride. Lechasseur wondered what it would take to diminish his self-confidence.

A group of figures clustered around Percival, bizarre, foreshortened from Lechasseur's perspective. They were taller than men, strangely proportioned and grotesque. Their movements were lithe and graceful, unimpeded by what he was at last coming to realise, with a paralysing horror, must be a heavier gravity than that of the Earth. The nearest figure turned a curious, flinty gaze upon him, and Lechasseur recognised the features that he had earlier seen haunting my own.

Desperate for any information about his present plight, he scanned the figure's details. The skin was smooth and pine-green, perfectly hairless even on the face and scalp. The physiognomy was broadly human, save for the eyes, of which there were several. These formed a ring about the head, spaced apart from one another by perhaps the width of three fingers, with a second half-ring, similarly spaced, running across the cranium like a crest. Positioned beneath the central eye, the nose was snout-like, the jaws wide and equipped, not with teeth, but with a pair of metallic ridges. The ears were the most animal feature, resembling those of a cow or a deer.

The figure's arms and legs were significantly more robust than those of *Homo sapiens*. The left hand was human in every respect, save for the fingernails which were again of a metallic cast. The right manipulatory organ was not a hand, but a cluster of fine tentacles resembling a sea anemone. The creature's broad shoulders and muscular waist seemed categorically to mark him out as a male of the species, and yet the round breasts and cleft pudendum implied the very opposite. The feet were large and flat, with toes so elongated as to mimic fingers. To Lechasseur's surprise, the thorny blades bent underneath the creature's soles as harmlessly as if they had been real grass.

Strangest of all, despite every characteristic marking this figure out as inhuman, many of which were elusive to define and yet profoundly unsettling, Lechasseur found himself convinced beyond rational doubt that he was looking at a man. To his uncomprehending gaze, the creature was not merely male; not merely human in broad outline; not merely, as he obviously was, an intelligent being: but actually a man, an individual of the race of mankind. If this was what men had become, Lechasseur wondered appalled, how far into the future had Percival brought him? Ten thousand years? A million? Further still?

Darkness encroached upon Lechasseur's exhausted vision as the man reached out and, in a grave gesture of welcome that was wholly human, placed a hand on Percival's shoulder. Calmly, the boy nodded and declared, 'I think I understand now.' The other figures, fading now, closed in around Percival, touching him, murmuring, as against his will Lechasseur's mind recapitulated its earlier retreat into oblivion.

III: MEN AND SUPERMEN

1. AT THE RETREAT

The afternoon succeeding the arrival at my house of Violet and Emily was spent in frantic planning and debate, although the latter term implies a kind of balanced exchange of ideas with one's equals which Violet's precocity could never have allowed. I had had ample opportunity to observe during my acquaintance with Percival how that gifted young man, while by no means always in the right on any given matter, was nevertheless usually able to muster arguments cogent enough to demolish any reasoning offered by myself, however conclusive the latter might seem to me.

In just this way, all my and Emily's opinions were as chaff before the gale of Violet's resolve, which was to return to the Retreat post-haste with us both in tow. 'Percival can look after himself,' she insisted, 'and it sounds like your Honoré's used to doing the same, Emily. There's nothing we can do for them here and now, anyway.' We had agreed that, provided Percival and Lechasseur did not become separated in whichever era it was that they had reached, they would be able to return to the present whenever they chose. I considered this reassurance to be both contentious and conditional, but Violet had little patience with my reservations.

'There's more important things at stake,' she said. 'I know I didn't let slip to those soldiers about the Retreat, and you say you didn't either. But we don't know who else they might contact. You're not the only person we've stayed in touch with out in the normal world, you know, Erik.' (This came as news to me.) 'We know you're loyal, but you're only *Homo sapiens*. Most of you couldn't hold up for half-an-hour under real torture, even for the sake of your own families. That's a scientific fact, I'm afraid. I can't see you sticking it out any longer than that for *us*.' Her mouth made a *moue*.

Violet's principal concern was with the defence of the Retreat against the possible advent of the military hunters. 'We haven't got anywhere else to go,' she admitted. 'Sometimes, when some of us are on our own, out in your world, they *vanish*. We never find out where they go to. But at the Retreat we've always been safe. We thought, if you people ever did threaten us there, we could go and join one of the other colonies overseas, but they've got their own problems now. We didn't think you were capable of such a co-ordinated campaign – more fools us.'

By peering out from behind my upstairs curtains, I had confirmed our observer's identity as that of St John Spears' rather thuggish chauffeur. He sat in a parked car, less ostentatious than the Rolls-Royce which he had been driving earlier in the day, and wore incongruous earmuffs which doubtless hid a pair of the protective earpieces. We could not rely on Violet's talent to conceal us from him, and so, when Violet had with impatient magnanimity allowed me the time to pack some clothes and to advise my wife by telephone to stay with her cousins for the moment, we made our egress by the route which Violet and Emily had used previously. Had any of my neighbours happened to be watching their gardens on that fine June afternoon, they would have espied a respectable novelist being assisted by two young women in an undignified scramble over his own back fence.

Violet had vetoed my suggestion that we obtain the use of a car from one of these same neighbours: she said that she had a contact in the immediate vicinity from whom she might borrow a motor without the need for convoluted explanations. The vehicle turned out to be a handsome brand-new Morris Oxford, into which Emily and I unquestioningly climbed. So unused had I become to dealing with the supernormals and their dismissive approach to conventional morality, that we were passing through Richmond before it occurred to me that

Violet had simply appropriated the first vehicle she found in the nearby streets.

There was something mesmerising about the young girl's presence which discouraged such doubts and questions: a personal magnetism which had little to do with her more esoteric capabilities, and more in common with that faculty of charisma which marks out certain individuals of our own species as natural mob-rulers. Violet was not a leader among the supernormals: insofar as that concept had any meaning for them, the honour went to Percival. Violet merely partook of this, as of so many other faculties, in a deeper degree than almost any normal human being.

I have already implied that the location which I described in *The Peculiar* as that of the Retreat was an invented one: indeed, in positioning Percival's communitarian settlement on a tropical island, I was indulging myself in a wilful fancy. That there were compelling reasons for obfuscation had been evident to me even then, hence the publication of that account as a novel, rather than as the memoir it was in reality. As the astute reader will have guessed, the colony was in fact not far from London on the global scale, and it will simplify the telling of my current tale considerably if, rather than maintaining the cumbersome pretence, I merely reveal that the supernormals' sanctuary was prosaically situated on an isolated farm in North Wales. Our plan was to overnight somewhere near Shrewsbury, and to reach the farmstead at some time around luncheon the next day.

As our journey progressed, both Emily and Violet became increasingly pensive and silent, a fact which I ignorantly attributed to concern for their friends, perhaps compounded in Emily's case by a bewilderment at the bizarre situation in which she had found herself so unexpectedly embroiled. In fact it later transpired that Violet, even while she was driving us north-westward with a rapidity and skill that many a motorist would have envied, was communing mentally with the community at the Retreat, preparing it for our arrival. As for Emily, fantastical occurrences and situations were her and Lechasseur's stock-in-trade, as I would shortly discover. Her sombreness arose, she would tell me, from brooding on the crisis which faced the supernormals.

As an unusually gifted individual herself, she was perhaps better able to empathise with these miraculous specimens of a new humanity than I, in whom admiration had always been tempered with a certain alienation. There was also the question of her amnesia.

'I understand how they must feel, at least a bit,' she confided in me at one point in the afternoon's journey, when the pair of us had prevailed upon an unwilling Violet to make a necessary break for comfort's sake. 'I know what it's like to find yourself in a world that has no place for you, where you won't belong however hard you try to fit in. You try to build yourself a sanctuary, and it's torn down again each time. As for these soldiers ... well, I've never experienced that kind of persecution, I'm glad to say. Hunting someone down, trying to wipe out a whole race, just because you're scared of what they can do ... what kind of mentality do you think it takes, Erik, to give yourself over to that kind of blood-lust?'

I shook my head. The same problem had been exercising me since I spoke with Percival. 'It's man's brute nature breaking through, I suppose,' I said. 'These men believe that *Homo peculiar* threatens their lives, and the life of their whole species. An elderly and feeble lion will fight with all its fading strength against a vigorous youngster who tries to take over the pride. It's a return to the basic imperative of evolution: to kill or be killed. In this case, though, it's hopeless. These children are mankind's future, and there's no sense in resisting the fact.'

Despite our earlier agreement, Violet decided without consultation that she would drive on through the night, allowing us to reach the Retreat by morning. She insisted that her constitution was more than adequate to the prolonged mental and physical exertion which this would entail. Emily and I slept fitfully and uncomfortably in the Oxford's leather seats, and I awakened, stiff and cold, to behold those majestic Welsh mountains, lonely and grey, limned by the orange glow of the dawn sun.

An hour later, we were with Violet's friends at the Retreat. The community occupied a collection of farm buildings, rude but robust in construction, which had been adapted in various ways towards the comfort of their new occupants. When the property had fallen (by what means I had never discovered) into Percival's hands, it had been abandoned and derelict. Since then, however, thanks to his hard-won agricultural knowledge and the combined ingenuity of his friends, it had become a working farmstead whose resources were perfectly capable of supporting the thirty or so European specimens of *Homo peculiar* whose home it had become, and who now gathered round us like a troupe of apes, jabbering and gabbling in several tongues.

There was loveliness in the crowd, but there was also hideousness. A typical member of the superior species appears to our eyes malformed and misshapen, although certain fortunate individuals attain an equally striking, if otherworldly, beauty. Frequently, the bodily deviations which these individuals sport turn out to be organic augmentations which allow their bodies to function more perfectly, improving in practical if not aesthetic terms on the design which nature has imposed upon normal men. To my unsophisticated gaze, however, this mob of near-humanity which teemed about us was reminiscent of those grotesque depictions of crowds in the paintings of certain of the Flemish masters: a catalogue of ugliness and deformity which nonetheless, when viewed in full and with a dispassionate eye, achieves a heterogeneous harmony which may indeed be considered beautiful.

When Violet, who seemed insolently fresh and rested after her exhausting labours, had greeted her friends, we were taken into the communal refectory to be fed. Neither Emily nor I had eaten since lunch-time of the previous day, and we partook gratefully of what was offered before we were presented to the community as a whole.

2. EMILY AND FREIA

Many inhabitants of the Retreat I had known already from Percival's early efforts to assemble his community together: some of them, indeed, had been my house-guests at one time or another. I immediately recognised Bridget, the first member of his own species whom Percival had met; Jimmie, the mathematical and musical prodigy who had caused such a sensation in London society eight years before, and who had been Percival's intimate in the latter's earliest, headiest days of sexual experimentation with his own kind; and sundry others. Jelena, the Russian girl who had been able to speak forty languages fluently by the age of twelve, and had become the fourth of the original founders of the community, was like Percival away from the Retreat on some unspecified errand.

All were of course older by several years than when I had known them, and they had begun to show those strange anomalies of the ageing process which are also typical of the supernormal strain. Jimmie, for instance, who was twenty-three, was already grey and balding, though his physique was that of a rather chubby eighteen-year-old. Bridget, the oldest of the founding members, appeared still in the transitory stages of puberty; while I would discover on Jelena's return that she, the youngest, had become by any standards a very beautiful young woman. Each greeted me cordially, but with a reserve which I had not encountered in them before. They were becoming wary of the outside world and its interventions in their lives.

Others of the community were unknown to me, and all, of course, were strangers to Emily. Some time was taken up in introducing the two of us to various members of the Retreat. From the abstracted air with which these youngsters told us their life stories, I suspected that a psychic conference was in progress, precipitated by Violet's arrival. The tension of it filled the atmosphere around us, yet it excluded us so entirely that Emily, I believe, remained unaware of its existence.

Some of the tales the newcomers told were fascinating, however. Pedro, a gangly, stammering Spanish youth of nearly seven feet tall, shyly confessed that he was also in excess of two hundred and fifty years old: he had simply ceased ageing at fifteen, and had spent most of his life as a novice in monasteries across Europe, moving on at intervals of a decade or so when his fellows grew wary or superstitious concerning his prolonged youthfulness. Although his protracted and cloistered existence had brought him great learning, in quickness of intellect and in imagination he was somewhat the inferior of most of the supernormals, and they made rather a pet of him.

There was a Greek boy, baptised Nikolas but usually addressed as 'Argos', who illustrated vividly the frequent utility of these so-called deformities of the supernormals. He possessed a cluster of additional eyes, half-a-dozen in number, which was located in the rear of his cranium. Although smaller than usual and lacking in eyelids, these orbs functioned perfectly well; and even when 'Argos' slept, which he did face-downward in one of the communal dormitories, they would swivel in their anterior sockets, following any movement in the room.

I was surprised to find among these friends of Percival and Violet one whom I had known by repute in the outside world. Mary O'Rourke had been a child-medium, of fragile and unhealthy appearance, who had caused a great stir when her devoutly spiritualist parents had brought her to England a few years previously. Her evidences of communication with the spirits of the dead were so outrageous, and yet so substantial, that an eminent scientist had taken it upon himself to 'de-bunk' them. After much study, he had finally confessed himself baffled as to what trickery the Irish girl was using, and shortly afterwards he had retired from public life.

Mary informed me that in fact her post-mortem communications had been entirely genuine. I knew that several of the supernormal children, following the death of a close family member, had believed that they remained in contact with some nebulous 'presence' of the deceased. Being sceptical by nature and by training, they usually attributed what for others might have been a source of comfort to the sheerest wishful thinking on their part. It seemed, however, that the particular form of Mary's religious upbringing, in which the souls of the departed had been routinely invoked, had caused her to develop the same faculty to a very much higher degree. She had come to realise that her skills were not proof of the survival of the soul, but rather a crude form of astral time-travel, in which she journeyed mentally into the past and came into direct psychic contact with the minds of those who were, according to the way we understand time, long dead.

Once Mary had come under the protection of the Retreat, Percival had taken it upon himself to hone this skill of hers, with a view to soliciting information from the future. His intention was that Mary might be induced to make contact with the Percival of a year in the past; and that, the habit of such communication having once been established, Percival would then be able in the present to call upon the valuable knowledge of the Mary of a year hence. I gathered that, as yet, their success in this had been minimal.

The last inhabitant of the Retreat to whom we were introduced was the youngest; since so far, Violet informed us cheerfully, no attempt to breed a supernormal with another supernormal had resulted in viable offspring. 'I think you'll like Freia, though,' she said. 'She came to us off her own bat from Germany, two years ago. She's six.'

This was an exceptional accomplishment, to say the least, but Freia was an exceptional child. She was one of those members of the peculiar species whose divergence from the *Homo sapiens* norm resulted, not in ugliness, but in transcendent beauty. Her face, the still-chubby face of a young girl, was that of a sphinx or a proud angel, regarding the world with condescending fondness and indulgent malice in equal measure. It was an expression which reminded me profoundly of Percival's at the same age.

The child was in all respects proportioned as a normal girl of her age, although the plumpness of her limbs belied the strength of the muscle underneath. Her intelligence was prodigious, and she could converse as well in English as many native speakers of the language could as adults. Emotionally, however, she was still a child, with all the attendant insecurities thereof, and a child's weird insensitivity to the feelings of others. Freia spent some time studying the two of us, with eyes the crystal blue of Alpine gentian, before she spoke. In a piping, almost unaccented voice, she declared, 'Neither of you are the same shape as other people. Why is that?'

'What do you mean, Freia?' Emily asked her gamely, as Violet smirked. I knew from long and embarrassing experience the difficulties of dealing with the young of the superior species: one might not treat them either as a human adult nor as a child, for they were neither one's equal nor one's inferior. One could only address them as the individuals they were at any given time, a fact which required constant adaptation to their rapid mental development.

'You are like an amputee,' Freia told Emily with great precision. 'Your past and future have been sliced away. And you –' she turned those ice-blue eyes on me '– have two lives, and only one of them is yours. There is another person hiding inside you. I should like to study you both some more.' I was unsure whether she was referring to Emily and myself, or to me and my mysterious inhabitant.

Violet was smirking still. 'Quite the little catch, isn't she?'

'You see people's lives, don't you, Freia?' Emily asked gently. 'You can see the shapes they make, back and forward in time.'

Freia sighed heavily. '*Yes*,' she said with a child's exaggerated patience. 'What happened to you, that cut off your past like that?'

'I don't know,' Emily told her. 'I've never known.'

Solemnly the little girl absorbed this, nodding. 'I'm going to play with the dogs now,' she said.

'That's all right, Frey,' said Violet. 'You run along. We didn't make the connection until yesterday,' she told us as the German girl bounded merrily away. 'We thought Freia's perceptions were another aspect of that gift Mary has. But after what you told me about time-sensitives, she's obviously one of them. Percival's going to be chuffed.'

I thought of Percival, loose in time, his experiments with Mary instantly surpassed by that effortless symbiosis which made a channeller and a sensitive into their own time-machine. As a young boy, Dr Tremaine had told me, Percival had always seen the normal passage of time as an arbitrary and annoying restriction. He would demand, 'Why must I wait? Why can't I have it already happening now?' or 'What do you mean, it can't be helped? Why don't we just do it again, and do it right this time?' He saw time as just another limitation imposed by *Homo sapiens* on itself, like laws or language. In this instance his natural arrogance (which I confess had never needed much nourishment in order to flourish) had perhaps been nurtured by the instinctive feelings of a time-channeller.

'You see now, don't you?' Violet was asking us. 'I had to bring you both here to the Retreat so you'd see. What we've got here's too important and precious to be compromised by your people. When those soldiers arrive, there's going to be a struggle for survival. Our survival, not yours – we're not planning to put *Homo sapiens* in danger, yet.'

'What do you mean, not yet?' asked Emily.

Violet regarded her with cool appraisal. 'I mean,' she said, 'the time for that will come, one day. The future lies with us – us supernormals, I mean – and our children, when we have them. Poor old *Homo sapiens*' days are numbered. Of course some higher specimens of your race may be kept on – I'm sure you'll be very useful to us. But you can't be allowed to keep up your breeding. If you went on unchecked, in ten years there'd be three thousand million of you, perhaps ten thousand million in a century. We can't let that happen.'

I had heard this refrain before, many a time, from Percival. He had been ten, and ignorant of the existence of others of his kind, when he first reached this conclusion, and he had been implacable in it since.

'You've done well enough,' Violet said. 'Given your limitations, you've made a pretty good job of preparing our Earth for us. And it's not such a bad fate, really. Do you think Neanderthal man mourned his own passing, when he allowed our ancestors to supplant him?'

'I would imagine he did, yes,' said Emily stiffly. It was the same tone I had adopted with Percival on countless occasions.

'Well,' Violet allowed, 'perhaps. But that just shows how underdeveloped he was. In that little struggle, *Homo sapiens* was the more developed type, you see, and he acquitted himself admirably. The poor old Neanderthal should have been happy, seeing as his extinction was allowing a higher, more vivid form of life to take his place. And so should you be happy now – or in ten years, whenever the struggle comes. Come on, if you knew you were the lesser candidate for an important job, one which it was really vital to everybody got done properly, you surely wouldn't try to put yourself ahead of the other person, would you? It's a noble thing, to give way to those better than yourself.'

Emily did not appear at all convinced, and I remembered her concerns of the previous day. She had been shocked then at the idea of one people attempting to wipe out another; and I could not imagine that she would reverse her judgement merely because this boot was on the other foot. Still, I thought, she would come around eventually, as I had, and quietly accept our species' fate. In the end, all of us would have to come around: the supernormals would make quite sure of that.

3. THE OPINIONS OF GIDEON BEECH

Emily and I were not the only visitors from the mundane world whom the inhabitants of the Retreat were to receive that afternoon. At around four o'clock, the deliberations in which we, Violet, Bridget and Jimmie were embroiled were interrupted by the noise of a second motor-car approaching the site. 'Is it the soldiers?' Emily asked, in immediate concern.

'No fear of that,' said Violet scornfully. 'They'd never have got past the perimeter, not without making enough fuss that we'd know about it. It's just Lou and Jelena coming back with Giddy.'

This was not the first time that this mysterious 'perimeter' had been mentioned. It seemed that among the technical advances which had been provided by Percival, Jimmie and the other engineers of the community (these included, along with numerous labour-saving mechanisms, a highly advanced generator for powering the entire site from 'the absolute annihilation of matter', and a device which I understood to be called 'the terminal', whose function was not at that time explained to me) was a mechanical means of focusing, directing and controlling personal psychic energy, whether it be that of an individual or of a psychical grouping such as the Retreat itself.

The collective state in which the group-mind of the community had been able to aid Violet in her escape from the town-house, and incidentally to condemn her rescuer, was not habitual and required considerable mental effort to sustain. This mechanism provided a less burdensome, and potentially an everlasting, alternative. Over the years, certain of the supernormals had become adept at the use of their telepathic abilities for offensive purposes, the assault which Percival had earlier directed against Lechasseur being an example, and by the use of the new device the engineers had been able to automate the process.

The machine could not, of course, replicate the specific technique whereby Percival had adapted his attack to Lechasseur's personal vulnerabilities, but a mechanised assault might be overwhelming nevertheless, as the device was able to draw for its power on the combined psychic potentialities of the Retreat's entire populace. It was, as Jimmie had informed us blithely, solely Violet's presence in our car which had spared Emily and myself from 'having our brains blasted to bits as we went along.'

('I can't help wishing Percival was here, though,' the young man had admitted. 'He's the one who designed the damned contraption, and he's the one we'll be needing if repairs or adjustments are to be made.'

'He'll be back soon enough,' Violet had said. 'Those soldier boys won't know what's hit them, you'll see.')

On this subject of their scientific ventures the young people were unusually forthcoming, and I could only respect the trust which they were placing in Emily and myself as members of the normal species – even if certain of their hints as to the potentialities of their other devices seemed to me both intriguing and terrifying.

The supernormals had decided unanimously that in the current crisis their defences, strengthened as necessary, would have to suffice. The sole alternative, that of evacuating the Retreat, was judged to be altogether too risky. The children would be far too conspicuous if they travelled *en masse*, and too vulnerable if they proceeded in smaller groups. Besides, there was no other refuge to which they might escape.

'And who is Giddy?' I asked Violet. Jelena I knew, naturally, and I had already heard mention of Lou as her paramour.

'Ask a lot of questions, don't you?' Violet said pertly. 'You'll see soon enough.'

Just as earlier in the day the supernormals had crowded into the farmyard to greet our party as it arrived, so now they ran out to meet the approaching motor-car, whose occupants I had difficulty discerning in all the hubbub. When they finally emerged from the crowd, Jelena and the young person whom I assumed to be Lou were escorting a very elderly man, who was to all appearances of ordinary human origin. He was talking animatedly with such of the crowd as addressed him, and seemed infused with an energy which must have been altogether exceptional at his advanced age. He carried a stick, but his sprightly manner of walking suggested that he must have recourse to it but rarely. His eyes were bright, his high forehead lined, and he sported a square, methuselaic beard of wiry hair.

'Good Lord!' I exclaimed. 'Is that – that surely can't be Gideon Beech, the playwright?'

Violet was smug. 'We're gathering our friends together. Those we've got left, at least,' she added, more soberly.

'But he must be ninety if he's a day!' I protested.

In point of fact, Mr Beech, who has the distinction of being probably our most eminent living dramatist, was at that time ninety-three years of age, and has since turned ninety-four. He has been a prominent figure in the sphere of English letters for very nearly as long as I have been alive, and it is fully twenty-five years since he received the Nobel Prize for Literature.

I had had no idea that he was known to the supernormals, nor that they were interested in him. He had not been among the literati or the theatrical people with whom the young Percival had consorted during his brief time in London.

Mr Beech was conveyed into the rustic outbuilding, now hollowed out into a capacious and well-appointed refectory, where Emily and I had been conversing with Violet and the others. He took a seat at the head of the one long table, and gazed complacently about himself. 'Well then,' he said, addressing the room at large. 'This is a fine pickle you young people have got yourselves into.'

'Mr Beech,' I said. 'I had no idea that you were known here.'

He frowned at me. 'And who the devil might you be, laddie?' he asked.

Hastily I introduced myself, aiding his memory by mentioning that the two of us had corresponded once or twice on literary matters. 'And this is Miss Emily Blandish,' I added, trying and failing to remember when I might last have been addressed as 'laddie'.

He smiled at Emily. 'Charmed, m'dear. And Mr Clevedon, too. Well well. You write those novels full of stuff that's supposed to be some sort of scientific philosophy, don't you? Yes, Jelena told me you might be here.' (I could have wished that Violet had done me the like courtesy, but I did not say so.) 'It seems we're letting anybody in these days – I don't mean you, of course, young lady. Well, never mind.'

I recalled now, amidst a growing dismay, that a greatly inflated sense of his own importance to the world had always permeated Beech's writings. This spilled over into his public dealings, and had certainly stood as a prominent feature of our correspondence. His genius was doubted by none who were familiar with his work and field, but least of all by himself. Many contemporary critics considered him to be the greatest British dramatist since Shakespeare: Beech, however, had observed on more than one occasion that Shakespeare's claims to greatness had yet to convince him, and some of Beech's best-known plays were attempts to set the record straight on historical matters where he felt his illustrious predecessor had been in error.

Despite his arrogance and condescension, however, I had thought that I recognised in Gideon Beech a kindred spirit. Now I was revising that judgement.

'Quite right, Giddy,' Violet said patronisingly. 'It's Liberty Hall here. We're open to all – even ancient geniuses.' Beech smiled, acknowledging the gibe.

It did not take long for Beech to be apprised of the details of the particular crisis currently facing the supernormals. He asked perceptive questions, and made some trenchant points concerning the difficulties which might arise during the defence of the Retreat. Plainly, despite the venerable age which he had reached, his formidable intellect had not yet deserted him, and I came grudgingly to realise that the young people had made a very sensible choice in recruiting him to their cause.

Still, there was something incongruous about the tenor of his discourse, and it took me some time to put my finger on it. 'Well, then,'

Beech observed again, after some discussion, 'it looks like this may be the beginning of that cataclysm which we've been anticipating, my children. Tomorrow may well see us all embroiled in the deciding struggle of normal versus supernormal, man versus superman. I suppose that each of us here has the good sense to see whose part Life will take in such a conflict; with the exceptions perhaps –' (here he smiled and nodded) '– of Clevedon and Miss Blandish.' He beamed benevolently at the assembled company, and it struck me suddenly that Beech was conceited enough to count himself (surely erroneously!) among the supernormals' number.

I stared at him for several moments. Much of his face was hidden by that famously patriarchal beard, but he clearly had none of those aberrations of physiognomy which were the outward indications of the *Homo peculiar* type. Besides, save Pedro, he was six or seven decades older than the oldest of them.

'I'm not sure I follow you, Mr Beech,' Emily was saying. 'Are you saying that you think the children have a chance of *winning* against these soldiers? Not just surviving, I mean, but defeating them?'

'My dear young lady, that and more besides,' Beech said. 'The thing has all the inevitability of history. These children whom you see around you are the heirs to what little claim we have upon humanity. It is they, meek though they most assuredly are not, who shall very shortly inherit the Earth. Don't you agree, Clevedon?'

'I suppose that you believe them to have been purposely created for that end,' I said, 'by your blind Earth-goddess.' Like most of the reading public, I am aware that Beech follows an arcane and pseudo-scientific religion of his own devising, one which elevates the 'Will of Life' (a half-hearted personification of evolution, and evolution understood according to an arcane pre-Darwinian scheme, at that) to the status of a deity. According to Beech, the development of life is a self-directing process, in which this formless and half-conscious creatrix strives constantly to improve upon herself.

Certain critics, including the noted Christian apologist Prof John Cleavis, claim to have found a degree of sympathy between Beech's philosophy and my own, amounting to something like a unified dogma. In fact this perception could not be further from the truth.

While I see the universe, and the life within it, as incidentally a part of the creator, abstracted and detached as a prelude to being shaped objectively by that deity's conscious mind, Beech sees his deity as actively present in Life itself, engaged in a half-witted, animal struggle towards her own betterment. In my work I have endeavoured to show that Man, however noble in his own right, is ultimately all but irrelevant to the cosmical scheme, whereas Beech ignores the very likely possibility of life outside our solar system, and makes Man in his current incarnation, as the highest present achievement of the life-force, central to the whole plan of creation.

In this, Beech's supposedly scientific faith duplicates that very anthropocentrism which has been a cardinal mistake of those older creeds which he intends for it to overthrow. More disastrously still, in seeing life and spirit as the ultimate good and their negation as the ultimate wrong, he recapitulates their moral dualism. I have struggled in my own thought with this very beguiling error; but I always return to the conclusion that our human categories of 'good' and 'evil' are meaningless when applied to the deity: that our Creator combines in His nature both absolute good and what is in our terms absolute evil, and that our purpose as His creatures, whatever our feelings might be in the matter, is as much to suffer as to thrive.

'Oh, to be sure,' Beech said in answer to my objection, beaming. 'Created by the Will of Life to be sure, but indirectly. Their mundane creators are rather closer to home. The Will shall always find a way to express herself, and in the present instance she has chosen to speak through the medium of human folly. These children represent Man's tragic pride given form, for it is Man – the old, obsolete model – who inadvertently and foolishly has made them.'

His imparting of this news both astonished and unsettled me. Violet and the others received it with apparent calm, but I was sensitive to certain subtle clues of expression and posture which would have eluded one less familiar with the supernormals' company. Beech's declaration, whether it were truth or (as I could not help but suspect) a fiction devised in order to allow him to remain the centre of attention, was to them wholly new information.

Jelena, who seemed to have appointed herself as Beech's guardian, gave an exaggerated sigh. 'Out with it, please, Giddy,' she said. 'Stop being so mysterious, and tell us all you know.'

What it was that Gideon Beech knew, or claimed that he knew, I will now tell. Out of a basic consideration for my fellow-author I will try as best I may to represent the playwright's words verbatim; out of respect for my readers, however, I shall strip away the greater portion of Beech's tediously self-aggrandising commentary on his own part in affairs.

I must state now, though, that while his narrative made me profoundly uncomfortable, and while I felt extremely dubious about the philosophical gloss he placed upon it, I did not continue for long to doubt the specifics of his testimony.

4. THE 'HAMPDENSHIRE PROGRAMME'

'The ways are legion,' Beech said, 'in which Life progresses and betters herself, and her resources are boundless. Sometimes, though, the methods which she uses are thought too slow by her impatient children.

'You are not the first of your kind, naturally. Your friend Pedro has shown you that, and – well, modesty forbids. Life does as she pleases, and it has pleased her that sports such as yourselves should appear at intervals throughout mankind's history. Socrates was such a one, as was Gautama. Even that dabbler Jesus of Nazareth may have been of a similar type to some degree. But you, my children, represent the first time in the evolutional experience when a whole crop (and such a fine crop it is, too) of *Homo peculiar* has sprung up at the same historic instant (and such a critical instant!)

'You are all of you too young to remember the Great War which came before the last one, and which was meant to end all possibility of future war; except for Mr Clevedon, who perhaps like many among his generation remembers it too well. Millions of young men died in that conflict, torn to shreds by bombs, bullets or barbed wire; and many more returned to their homes convinced that killing a man was no very great thing, and that the problems of mankind might perhaps be solved by killing a great many men all in one go.

'It was an evil time for those of us who serve the cause of Life, and who value the spiritual unity of mankind over and above the petty claims of our temporal and temporary nation-states.

'Different kinds of men took away different lessons from that war. Those of us in all the nation-states who considered that our loyalties transcended whatever limited sense of place our tribal leaders might have tried to instil in us, made attempts to come together as citizens of the globe, and to co-operate towards ensuring that an atrocity such as the war could not easily occur again. Some of us felt that this could only be accomplished by establishing an international scientific elite, to guide the world's less educated classes; others looked forward to a unification of the religions of mankind; while others still held out hopes for the revolution of the proletariat.

'All of us understood that some form of comprehensive social planning, benevolent in its aims but ruthless when necessary in its execution, would be indispensable for the bringing-about of any such state of affairs. A few of us had the intellectual wherewithal to realise that such an ambitious end could be achieved by no less lofty a means than the remaking of human nature itself.

'The men who were in charge of the nation-states, by contrast, had come to a very different set of conclusions. Their belief – for in this regard the beliefs of those at the apex of power in every civilised country, thus-called, were identical – was that, if such a war were ever to recur, their own tribe must at all costs be the one that should prevail. To this end, these men set about strengthening their nation-tribes. They did this surreptitiously, knowing that if such a project were to succeed, it must be done in secret, away from the gaze both of their own war-weary populations and of the spies of other nations.

'Those programmes which they undertook revolved for the most part around acquiring new weapons, whether by discovery or invention. Naturally this required the aid of experts in all the applied sciences, the newest and most dynamic of these being the biological. The war itself had seen some hopeful innovations in the killing of men in large numbers by the application of the science of Life and, with a view to building upon such undoubted progress, the tribal governments each assembled, in deadly secret, the best of their biological experimenters.

'There was a surprising and felicitous correspondence between the ambitions of the nation-states and those of the aspiring internationalists. For one of the plans dreamed up severally but identically by the leaders of every nation was that of breeding improved fighting-men: soldiers who would fight with all the strength, cunning and valour of the heroes and demi-gods of old, whether the local avatars taken by these paragons were called Artorius, Siegfried or Paul Bunyan.

'There had indeed been some efforts in this direction both during the war and earlier, but they had not been successes, and their embarrassing products had usually been tidied neatly away out of sight. However, with the recent discovery of such sciences as that of eugenics, the authorities were hopeful that more satisfactory results might be obtained. To this end, the biologists were ordered to discover means of making supermen, although of course the tribal leaders thought that they were asking for super-Germans, super-Americans or super-Englishmen.

'Naturally a good number of these biological experimenters were members of that fledgling international confederacy which the scientists of all the nations had been working to establish. Some of them were members also of that more rarefied association to which I had myself the honour of belonging, which perceived the future hopes of mankind as lying wholly in the physical and mental betterment of the race.

'The scheme to breed the super-Englishman was known as "The Hampdenshire Programme", after one case of infantile prodigiousness so notorious as to have penetrated even the notoriously impregnable imagination of the mandarins of Whitehall. Many of the primary movers in this patriotic branch of the great global endeavour were known to me. I myself have not, alas, been taught biology formally, although my knowledge of the science is extensive. Even had I, however, I doubt that His Majesty's Government would have been keen on entrusting the future of our nation's fighting-men to one of my well-known radical sympathies. Nevertheless, on behalf of the more progressive of the international superhumanists, I acted as an extremely unofficial advisor to some of the individuals involved.

'For the members of that loose global federation, the plan of campaign could not have been clearer. The biological experts of every nation, co-ordinated clandestinely by individuals such as myself, would work together in a secrecy so absolute that not even the spy-services of the individual nation-tribes would be able to observe it. The specimens whom they would generate would be just as their paymasters requested, stronger, more cunning and braver than the best of humanity: and it would be these very qualities which would prevent them from falling under the spell of any lesser cause than that of Life herself.

'Thus they would become a single race of supermen: for surely a solitary superman, in the service of a single nation-state, fighting for one tribe's way of life against that of another, was an unthinkable absurdity.

'It sometimes happened that, for what were considered to be ethical reasons (for unhappily some of the subjects died or were permanently mutilated during the course of the experiments), particular operations were confined to isolated groups of natives in the colonies. Often, though, the subjects of the Hampdenshire experiments were British residents living in out-of-the-way places, who remained quite unaware of the higher plan in which they were participating. As I have said, the internationalists were obliged to be ruthless, and of course the rulers of the English nation-tribe did not have very many moral qualms about harming some of its members in order to make others function better.

'By the criteria of all the interested parties, however, the experiments were a dismal failure. Beyond a slight increase in muscle capacity which might have been down to exercise, and a minor advance in understanding which could easily have been achieved by attending evening classes, the young men and women experimented upon remained resolutely normal. By the late 1920s, not only the Hampdenshire Programme, but as I learned from my international contacts its sister projects in almost all the tribal nations, had been dismantled by those nations' governments.

'There, so we all believed, the matter rested: until, that is, our specimens began to breed.

'I see from your expressions that I am anticipated. Well, so be it. Each one of you (saving your presences, Clevedon, Miss Blandish) has one parent, or in rare cases two, who had been an experimental subject in the Hampdenshire Programme, or in one of the other identical projects which took place elsewhere.

'In a prosaic sense, you are the children of the Programme, and the creatures of the governments of mankind. The Great War showed us all that man's capacity to act as the guardian of this planet was tragically limited. You are the nation-tribes' fumbling and inept response to this revelation. And yet, through you, the Will of Life has chosen to speak far more eloquently. You represent the highest type to which that Will has yet aspired; and you will supersede humanity as readily as man the mastodon.

'The last two wars have seen the tribal states of *Homo sapiens* exterminating one another in unprecedented numbers. The next war will, I am certain, take that process to its natural conclusion: the final extinction, at your own infinitely versatile hands, of *Homo sapiens* himself.

'The leaders of the tribes know this, of course. They have been shocked to see their citizens give birth to gifted little monsters, and they have watched in horror as those monsters have grown into the supermen those leaders once thought themselves in need of, and whom now they fear above all else.

'These soldiers they have sent to harry you, my children, and your brethren elsewhere, are the arms and hands of the nation-tribes, making their last feeble effort to fight away the merciful surcease which you offer them. You must knock aside these failing limbs of theirs, not without compassion, and push the lethal needle home into their moribund flesh.

'Only then will your decrepit old parent, *Homo sapiens*, have that rest from his labours which he has so faithfully earned.'

IV: AN AMERICAN IN FUTURITY

1. IMPRESSIONS OF THE FUTURE

Honoré Lechasseur's memories of his sojourn in futurity are nebulous and partial, even now. He was dazed by his arduous journey through the ages, his mind inchoate and fragmented, and he had great difficulty in translating the images and sensations which he received into impressions which he was capable of understanding. In all likelihood, any man of our century, whatever his origins, would have experienced similar difficulties in adapting to that strange and distant epoch. There was too little commonality, too little which was shared, between the two worlds.

The reader may recall Mr H G Wells' time-traveller, and his frustration at his own failure to comprehend the future in which he found himself:

> Conceive the tale of London which a Negro, fresh from Central Africa, would take back to his tribe! What would he know of railway companies, of social movements, of telephone and telegraph wires, of the Parcels Delivery Company, and postal orders and the like?

Lechasseur was a Negro of the modern age, a native not of the African jungle but of a proud city of a highly developed nation. He had been already a passing visitor to other times both past and future, though rarely to any epoch greater than a century from our present. In this regard, he was indeed rather better prepared to interpret the phenomena of this remote futurity than you or I had been, or Mr Wells. Faced with the reality of it, however, his apprehension was quite as helpless as, I am nearly certain, would have been each of ours.

He believes that the time during which he remained there might have been counted in days, not in hours or weeks; but in that place the stars neither rose nor set, and the sky remained veiled in that obsidian twilight. As his body became accustomed to that world's crushing gravity, he found that he was able, first to stand and then to walk or at least shamble, although the process was an arduous one and he required frequent rest. His time-sensitive faculty was still deaf and blind, and he wondered if it had burnt itself out altogether.

There was no trace that he could see of Percival, nor of the pine-hued giant who had, so Lechasseur assumed, led the young man away. The plain on which he found himself continued for as far as he could spy in all directions, flat and spiked with the unwelcoming blades of 'grass'. The purple-black cliff which he had observed turned out to be the nearest side of a vast tapering tower, one of several which dotted the plain irregularly, the nature and purpose of which entirely eluded him. Sometimes he thought that these must be dwellings, at other times geological formations, or animal constructions like a termite mound. Their texture appeared something between chalk and candle-wax, and he even entertained the thought that they might be colossal plant growths. They were abuzz with swarms of birds, or perhaps large insects, depending on the structures' size.

All over the ground low cairns of earth and stones were scattered, towards a horizon which, he says, 'somehow seemed like it was too flat.' There were no trees, but instead stands of shrubs, coloured much like the grass, their leaves so closely-packed as to resemble a cauliflower. Lechasseur was famished, and he tried breaking off a part of one of these to eat. It was revolting, but he crammed it down.

Awkwardly, he stumbled across that unforgiving ground in the direction of the nearest of the giant edifices. He was in a feverish daze, and it dawned on him only gradually that he had been walking already for the best part of an hour. The construction, or creature, or whatever it might be, was scarcely larger than it had appeared from the place where he and Percival had made their landfall. The skies were cloudless, and without a background to the object Lechasseur had dramatically misjudged its scale: the outcrop was as big as or bigger than the Earth's highest mountains. The myriad specks that played about it must be gigantic flying things, the size of men or larger.

At this point there is a hiatus in his recollection of events.

The next experience that he is able clearly to remember is this: he was sitting in an area ringed with cairns, which was occupied by a small party of the otherworldly human beings. These were going about some incomprehensible business of their own, and ignoring Lechasseur's presence altogether. They had some items with them of around the size of wardrobes, which might have been plants or artefacts, or possibly the bony shells of living creatures. Each of these was somehow emitting coldness, as if it were an oven radiating heat. Lechasseur, who found the climate of this world oppressive (it was, perhaps, not greatly warmer than his native New Orleans, but after his years in London it came as a shock to his system), gratefully crouched down next to one of these and basked in its chill.

After a while, one of the human creatures took from a nearby cairn some chalky hemispheres, about the size of Lechasseur's two clenched fists. This man (if he was indeed a man, for as I will explain Lechasseur entertained some doubts as to his sex), opened up a tap or orifice in one of the cold objects, and filled these bowls in turn with the viscous, milky fluid which was thence secreted. (Lechasseur noticed that the individual used his anemonoid appendage to manipulate the delicate mechanism, and his more humanlike left hand to hold the grosser hemispheres: this, he would later discover, marked the general distinction in usage between the two organs.) The man then handed round the bowls to his fellows: indifferently and without any other acknowledgement of the black man's presence, he included Lechasseur in his rounds. The American said, 'Thanks – thank you very much,' but the company ignored him altogether. They were, between themselves, quite silent, either in no need of conversation, or carrying out their communication by ethereal means quite inaccessible to their guest.

The feeding of a stranger, which would have been instantly recognisable as a gesture of hospitality had it taken place at the hands of a previously undiscovered tribe in Borneo or Guinea, in this instance reminded Lechasseur of nothing so much as the putting down of food for a stray animal toward which one felt a humane duty, but which one hoped would not disrupt one's household by staying for too long. He felt intense gratitude nonetheless, for his body had rejected the piece of bush which he had eaten. He gulped hungrily at the draught.

His indifferent hosts were between eight and ten in number. In the stocky humanness of their shape they were broadly consistent, and most, though not all, possessed one of the specialised manipulating organs; otherwise, though, they were very diverse in appearance. Either the features which Lechasseur had previously observed were not universal to this race, or else this world's inhabitants were of many different species.

In height the party ranged from seven feet to ten or twelve, though whether its smaller members might be children or colossal pygmies, he could not say. Their facial features were extremely heterogeneous, although they were in similar degrees human and bestial, with an abstraction in their expressions which reminded Lechasseur of the funerary angels which ornament the cemeteries of his home city. Most had more than two eyes, the arrangements and dispositions of which varied. Most, too, had ears and noses which seemed more like those of animals than of men, although the creatures which they recalled to his mind were as dissimilar as horses, bats and sea-lions. Their skin tones and textures were similarly divergent, no two alike: some of the group were bald, others velvety or shaggy; some sported vestigial scales, or were wrinkled like tree-bark; and the hues of their skin ranged from chryselephantine to a marbled blueish-black quite unlike Lechasseur's own complexion.

In sexual characteristics, too, they seemed wildly assorted, more so than might be explained by our familiar Earthly sexes. All of them had frames which seemed in general delineation clearly male or female; yet some of the apparent men had breasts like those of women, and some of the apparent women lacked them. While every one of them was naked, none had visible sex organs. (Lechasseur would discover later that, while these existed, and in multiple forms, they were stored inside the pudendal cleft when not in use, becoming apparent only when engorged.) He somehow gained the impression that these variations represented those of many sub-sexes, and that the simple 'he's and 'she's which the English language bestows upon her subjects would suffice to convey but the crudest impression of these people's sexualities.

All of this Lechasseur pondered as he drank his milky broth. The liquid was both creamy and salty, and very rich: and despite his appetite, he found that he was able to finish barely half of the meal. It soon became apparent also that it possessed a strong intoxicating element. He shortly became very sleepy, and despite his fears as to the intentions these men and women of the future might have for him, he found himself entirely unable to remain awake. When he came to himself, minutes or hours later, the people were gone, along with all their equipment.

Lechasseur's remembrance of what, insofar as he could measure time at all, he judges to have been the next few days, is a confusion of unrelated impressions and incidents.

He remembers examining an artefact, large as a house and shaped like a conch-shell, but with a satiny surface which would quiver disquietingly when touched. He heard what sounded like voices coming from deep within, although he knew that the people he had seen had not spoken aloud amongst themselves. He was unable to find any means of ingress, and his pocket-knife could make no impression upon the resilient flesh.

At one point he came upon a group of men and women who had taken root in the soil of that treeless plain, and whose heads had sprouted profusions of leaf-like blades which they angled towards the brightest of the pale stars. They seemed deeply asleep, their many eyes so sunken into their skin-bark as to resemble the knots of a tree-trunk. Lechasseur felt that they were enrapt in serene contemplation: indeed, he gained from them a sense of placidity so overwhelming that he fell onto his knees, longing to sink his own fingers and toes into that loam, and to soak its moisture up into himself.

He spent some time within that grove of tree-men in a reverie, resting at last from his recent exertions. Soon, though, he found himself unnerved by their tranquillity, into which he felt himself drawn ever deeper. He sensed that, through the influence of the tree-men, he was approaching an absorption of his soul into a thing vaster than itself, the placid vegetative consciousness of the plants; and through them perhaps something more, a union with the cosmic source of life itself. In terror, he tore himself from the ground (where he had not, indeed, taken root, but which he found more difficulty in leaving than might be accounted for by the heavy gravity alone) and took flight, stumbling in headlong panic from that place.

Eventually there came the incident which returned to Lechasseur the strength with which to gather the scattered embers of his mind, and stoke them into flame. He was resting in the lee of a kind of megalithic stone, although the chalky surface was ambiguously bone-like in texture. He was becalmed in those sweltering doldrums of half-waking consciousness which had over the past days become his habitual mental state, and he did not register the purposeful approach of some heavy footsteps, until a deep, familiar voice spoke his name. Scrambling to his feet, Lechasseur turned to see the giant man, green-skinned and woman-breasted with a crown of blinking eyes, whom he had met on his arrival.

The Negro's first, wild instinct was to flee. This creature terrified him, not because it was alien to him, but because it was more fully human than any human being he had known. The fear which Lechasseur experienced was at once instinctive and profound: it was the trepidation of an unwieldy island animal, long established in its comfortable habitat, beholding for the first time the predator introduced by mankind to its isolated paradise. It was the lower organism's fear of the higher, the weaker for the stronger. Just so must the Neanderthal man have felt, when the first warriors of the Cro-Magnon tribes strode onto his land and raised their spears in territorial challenge.

'Honoré,' the man said again, and held out his five-fingered hand.

I have stated that Lechasseur was an exceptional specimen, and so he proved now. Not only was he able to subsume that very fear which had threatened to master him, but he was capable of examining it coolly enough to recognise its biological origins. Still more impressively, he realised at once that there could be one course alone which might allow for his survival in this world, surrounded by these proud supplanters of his own kin. It was the same strategy as had been employed millennia before by the ancestors of the dogs and cats, in adapting to the ever-broadening encroachments of humankind.

Obediently, he took the giant's hand. The green man turned his gaze upon the standing stone, and with a sound like shredding silk it split asunder, to reveal a bony funnel leading darkly downward. Together, he and Lechasseur stepped into the inside of the world.

2. THE STORY OF SANFEIL

I suppose that I must now address an issue which, during the foregoing, will have impressed itself forcefully upon those of you who are familiar with my previous writings. For this future which I have been depicting, the future which was described to me by Lechasseur, shares many of its most singular ingredients (the gravity; the towers; the heterogeneity and the paradoxically statuesque frames of its predicted humanity) with that outlined in certain of my novels, where it is supposed to be perceived in his mystical visions by my fictitious narrator.

I am sure that some impatient minds among you have already ascribed this to a final cataclysmic failure of imagination on my part. Others, willing to accept *The Peculiar* (a tale set in the present and describing mostly familiar characters and situations) as having had a basis in reality, are doubtless aggrieved to find yourselves the victims of an obvious hoax, now that I have revealed my altogether more incredible contention that my fantasies of future history, with all their weird and outlandish detail, have similar grounds in veracity.

In fact, as I shall shortly explain, the reason that my reflections of this distant future have turned out to be so improbably accurate is because they were vouchsafed to me, unconsciously as far as I myself was concerned, by a source familiar at first hand with that very future. Although I myself have been convinced that my Coming Men were a fiction, quite as certainly as I knew Percival and his friends to be a reality, nevertheless in making such a distinction I was altogether mistaken.

The name of Lechasseur's new companion, as nearly as it can be rendered by our vocal apparatus, was Sanfeil, and he was a student of his people's very distant past. He had scrutinised the dark years of our long-expired century for a span equivalent to many of our generations. It was, however, but one subdivision of his proper field of study, which was the whole history of the genus *Homo*.

He had been alive for tens of millennia, and in his time he had been such as we might ignorantly call philosopher, scientist and priest. He had five wives, most of whom he saw only a few times in a decade, and one of whom had suckled at his breast when an infant. He had taken many shapes: had spent some hundred years as a flying man, soaring across the skies of that world, and beyond, into the abyss between the planets; had taken his turn, when a callow and idealistic youth of a scant few centuries, among the tree-men as they contemplated the mysteries of the stars; had swum with fish-men in the nutritious oceans of that world, and crept with worm-men deep beneath its soil.

He used his own life-energy as you or I would use a tool, bending it to his will as effortlessly as we might switch on or off an electric light. By use of it he could reshape his body or his environment, and through it he had brought his innately rebellious spirit into harmony with his fellow men and with the group-mind of his world. In spirit he had embarked on lengthy journeys into space, consorted across its immense distances with alien humanities, and addressed as his equals the proud and fiery spirits of the stars. He worshipped, as did all his people, the Creator of the Universe, whom they envisaged as an artist, working with the limitlessly graduated shades of good and evil for His palette, and as a scientist, dispassionately refining His creation through generation after generation of experiments.

He was but one, and not among the most distinguished, of a race of men some hundred thousand million of whom populated that great globe as sparsely as oases in a desert.

All this Sanfeil conveyed to Lechasseur as they walked together through that chalky tunnel, towards what destination the American could not guess, although the other gave him to understand that he had come particularly in order to fetch the Negro thither.

Although Lechasseur is insistent that Sanfeil spoke aloud when he first said Lechasseur's name, as he had earlier addressed Percival, he maintains that the majority of this conversation took place without the necessity of speech. While Sanfeil could certainly make himself understood perfectly in our country's and century's vernacular (he would do so later), he was also able to imprint ideas directly onto the other man's mind. Some of these ideas took the form of words. Sometimes Sanfeil's thoughts appeared to him as images, or as experiences interpolated between his own memories. The Negro found himself, as he said later, 'drowning in his mind. He was pouring so much of himself into my head, it was as if what there was of me in there was being flooded out.'

Speaking to Sanfeil in his soft accented English, Lechasseur attempted to deflect this torrent of information, diverting its flow with questions of his own. Sanfeil was patient enough, although Lechasseur formed the impression that it took much effort for him to respond within a range of thinking which the American might understand. Lechasseur asked about the history of that world, and what its connection was with that of his own sphere: hoping, though without any great degree of confidence, that his surmise that they were in the remote future would turn out to have been mistaken.

Sanfeil answered, certainly, but whether by design or no the details of the stories he told – of mankind making for himself new tyrannies, new soviets and sodalities; of man's manifold reinventions of his species, of his growth and evolution; of the eventual destruction of the planet of his birth, and his migration to that artificial globe, constructed from the raw material of the solar system's outer worlds, on which he had at last perfected a utopia of total unity, and on whose leaden surface Lechasseur now stood – would vanish from the black man's recollection the instant the latter returned to his native time, leaving him with but the image of an ancient tapestry, all save the vividest of its rich colours long since faded to a dim and dusty grey.

Sanfeil told him other things, however, and these Lechasseur was able to retain. The giant explained the techniques used by his kind to mine the past for information, the chief of which was to observe events directly, through the minds of those who had experienced them.

Historians like himself used the long-vanished consciousnesses of others as windows upon their sundered worlds and times. Sanfeil informed Lechasseur that I was myself one of his favourite subjects, and that he had already monitored my life from birth to death, experiencing through me the quality of life in the late nineteenth and early twentieth centuries of the Christian era. It was, as Lechasseur and Percival before him had surmised, Sanfeil's time-line which the two of them had perceived underlying my own, on that June night long aeons previously, and by which they had been towed into his far-flung present.

A portion of Sanfeil's consciousness, as he now explained to Lechasseur, resided inside my person even while the two of them conversed. As they traversed those subterranean tunnels, a shoot or scion of Sanfeil's mind was still beholding through my self the events of those June days of 1950: my flight with Violet and Emily, my arrival at the Retreat and my introductions to Mary and Freia; my encounter with Gideon Beech and his story of the Hampdenshire Programme.

Through me, long since, Sanfeil had observed Percival's adolescence; and through me he had done his best to foster the young man's exceptional potential, somewhat superior as it might be considered to that of those dull man-apes, myself included, who surrounded him. For in history Sanfeil was no mere impotent observer. He might, even at such a remove in time and space, exert an influence upon my thoughts and actions. He had spent his time not solely in detached study, but also in industriously working beneath the threshold of my own awareness, to effect such results as he and his fellows considered desirable. These aims included (so, at least, I must conclude) the writing of my novels *The Coming Times* and *Men of the Times*.

In producing these books of mine (as in certain other actions of my life including, I can only assume, committing this final tale to paper now), I have been obeying the impenetrable will of a being who, though he shall be our inaccessibly remote descendant, will have motives and goals of his own: motives quite at odds with those which we now honour, and goals opposed to those which we hold sacred.

I fear that I do not find this a thought by which I may be greatly comforted.

3. SANFEIL AND PERCIVAL

It is for these reasons that I consider myself justified in employing my knowledge of that epoch, remote and mediated though it is, in presenting to my contemporaries the intimate experience of it which Honoré Lechasseur has recounted to me. In doing this I am aware of a substantial risk that I will end up misinterpreting my Negro friend's testimony.

Although the future which I have described in my novels (but for which it appears that I may no longer take the least imaginative credit) is as consistent and comprehensible a world as the domain presented in a fiction must perforce be, I believe that my far-future observer and controller will have had no choice but to simplify his understanding of that world, in order to render it consistent with our limited habits of twentieth-century, *Homo sapiens* thought. It may well be that every word I have written in *The Coming Times* and *Men of the Times* is, literally, false: however, I can only assume that these words in their totality must give, not indeed an accurate description of that future, but rather a faithful impression of it.

Faced with these alternatives, of remaining true on the one hand to the mystified perplexity which characterises Lechasseur's own account, or on the other of imparting the remainder of his experiences as if they had taken place within that child's painting of the future which is as much as our under-developed minds have been considered ready for, I have opted, not without reservations, for the latter course.

The artefact which Lechasseur and his guide had entered was the outlying root-system of one of those massive structures which protrude above the plains in that epoch like the ribs of the world. These colossal buildings of the Coming Men are grown from super-strengthened materials which are indeed of distantly animal, even human, origin, but which have had such liberties taken with their germ-plasm that they retain few recognisable characteristics of our Earthly fauna. After a long period of walking under the ground, the two men arrived at a region where the bony substance of the channel gave way to fibrous walls of more resilient material.

Throughout their journey, the physical relationship between the two of them had impressed uncomfortably upon Lechasseur a comparison with the ratio of sizes we observe between a parent and her child; although Sanfeil could only have been an immensely distant progeny of the American's contemporaries, and not even his own descendant, Lechasseur himself being childless. He found that being led by the hand by the giant aroused in him certain deep childhood associations, so that his natural terror coexisted most unsettlingly with a strange feeling of comfort.

At this boundary between the types of building tissue, Sanfeil halted. He made no outward sign, but must have conveyed an instruction telepathically to the materials around them, for at once the walls closed in upon them like a womb, and bore them up into the body of the edifice. Abruptly Lechasseur's already onerous weight was doubled, and his legs failed him, pitching him ignominiously to the spongy floor. For the next minutes his whole concentration was occupied with the effort of breathing, and he was only peripherally conscious of their conveyance coming to a giddying stop, and its muscular walls retracting into the floor of a much larger chamber. With one huge hand beneath each of Lechasseur's arms, Sanfeil helped the American to stand. The Negro recoiled instinctively from the squirming of the green man's tentacular appendage.

The atrium to which the building's internal workings had directed them was vast, shaped very like a chamber of the human heart, and illuminated by patches of purple phosphorescence. This light was lurid to Lechasseur's eyes, but the spectrum perceived by the optical organs of those future men is not like that apprehended by our sight. Lechasseur and his guide stood in one of those giant omnicompendious libraries of the Coming Men, although our term 'library' scarcely begins to comprehend the multiple social and cultural functions of these sites: to us it might have seemed market-place, church, lecture-theatre and laboratory rolled into one.

It might remind us also, as it did Lechasseur, of a botanical or zoological gardens, for the knowledge of the Coming Men is kept, not in the short lived medium of cloth and paper, but in the lineages of living creatures, their germ-plasm artfully manipulated so that they live lives both long and fertile. The more animal-like of these living 'books' secrete bodily fluids which are ingested by the scholars of the Coming Men (and all of the latter who are allowed to live beyond infancy become scholars at one time or another in their vastly extended lives); those which more closely resemble plants produce leaves or spores which may be eaten. Thus the knowledge which we would gain from scanning a book's pages is encoded within the bio-chemical composition of these foods, and the tongue of each 'reader', which is a perceptual tool as incisive and penetrating as our own eyes, translates this information into words, images or memories.

Naturally, none of this was known to Lechasseur, who merely observed that he was being led past what seemed to him a monstrous menagerie let loose in an ornamental garden, the total making up a wild profusion of colours, scents and textures. The chamber's fleshy walls were composed of cubby-holes, their function analogous to that of library carrels. Many of these were occupied by members of Sanfeil's race who sat or stood or knelt about their diverse tasks, the greater number of which were entirely incomprehensible to Lechasseur.

As I have said, these halls are endowed with functions which would seem to us very diverse; although to the understanding of the Coming Men they are all of a piece, and it is only to our ignorant minds that they appear muddled. Lechasseur was startled to see a knot of five or six persons, surely juvenile members of the species, who were engaged in some form of group sexual act beneath the vegetable creatures' broad flesh-leaves. The American was startled by the sight of one boy's intricate sexual apparatus as it blossomed forth from his abdomen. He gritted his teeth and followed his giant guide, until shortly they arrived at one particular nook, in which Percival was seated.

Lechasseur thought at first that the young man was attacking him once again; for the supernormal youth launched himself toward the American quite as precipitately as he had done on the previous occasion when they had met. To Lechasseur's surprise and discomfiture, however, Percival embraced him, clinging to his clothes and sobbing like a child. Confused, the Negro found himself looking to Sanfeil for guidance, and thought for a moment that he detected in that inscrutable countenance something akin to grim amusement. Supporting most of Percival's exaggerated weight, Lechasseur struggled over to a bench, a cartilaginous excrescence which protruded from the wall, whereon the boy had earlier been seated, and helped him to sit down once more. Sanfeil crouched opposite them, his powerful limbs splayed like those of a gigantic ape. Again he gave no outward signal, but at once a circle of muscular tissue drew inward around the entrance, so as to isolate their small nook from the greater chamber outside.

Lechasseur realised that Percival was trying to communicate with him: the young man's sobs had become words, coughed out like air from a bellows. 'Said I was – obsolete,' Percival was gasping, 'primitive. No better – than animals. No better – than you. A fossil – curiosity – a missing – link.'

Like Emily, Lechasseur had been ignorant of the presence of *Homo peculiar* among the populace of his own time. Before Emily's meeting with Violet, the species had not overtly appeared on the lengthy roster of queer phenomena with which the two investigators had come into contact. Since the American's mental balance had returned to him, however, he had been mentally comparing the anatomies of the men of this distant future with those aberrations of appearance which his erstwhile assailant had displayed. Percival's words seemed to confirm his earlier conclusions, and he thought that he understood (which is not to say that he felt any inclination to sympathise with) the boy's conspicuous distress at being placed in the same category with himself.

Sanfeil spoke, this time in the articulate voice of his body and in calm, accentless English. He said, 'We thought that we could help him to adjust, to live among us in our time instead of being sent back to your own to die; but we were wrong. He feels all of your alienation,

Honoré, but in his case it is immeasurably magnified by the sensibility of the common ground between him and ourselves. He cannot live with our honest opinion of his worth, and we cannot, will not perjure our understandings for his sake. He must go back: you, Honoré, must show him how to take you back.'

Lechasseur's temporal perceptions had been quiescent since his abrupt departure from London, and he had almost given up hope of their returning. On seeing Percival, however, it was as if they had been instantly re-calibrated. The young man's 'flesh-worm' presented itself to him, stretching a few days back into the past, before becoming attenuated and vanishing into the immense abyss of history. The present body of the supernormal youth was still, to Lechasseur's perceptions, interwoven with those threads of red, binding him to what was now their present like an insect in a web. Sanfeil's life was also perceptible, sturdy and ponderous as an oak, with roots and branches spreading into past and future. Even the edifice surrounding them had its own temporal presence, long-lived and no less alive than the others.

Lechasseur took Percival's hand, and tried to concentrate upon the depths from which their own time-traces had emerged and into which one single root of Sanfeil's time-tree plunged, but the young man pulled away from him. With an effort that was evident in every lineament of his face, Percival composed himself sufficiently to ask, 'Why must I die?' Sanfeil returned his belligerent glare indifferently, and Percival elaborated: 'You said I must be sent home to die, Sanfeil. Why?'

Sanfeil shrugged, a perfectly human gesture. 'All men die, Percival,' he said. 'Even your people die. Even my own.'

'That isn't it, though,' the boy persisted. 'You know something about *me*. About my ... not my future I suppose. About what was waiting for me, back then in the past.'

Sanfeil seemed to consider this, although he might as easily have been rapt in the contemplation of the mysteries of the cosmos, or observing that very event in the distant past of which the young man spoke. At length, he bowed his head and opened his mind; and once again a torrent of images and experience was flooding into Lechasseur's bruised awareness.

4. A DISTANT VIEW OF HISTORY

Honoré Lechasseur does not know, and I had no opportunity to enquire, in what form Percival perceived the voluminous quantity of information which Sanfeil then imparted to them both. I am aware (for this Lechasseur himself explained, falteringly and at length, to Emily and myself as we drove back to London together) that the American experienced it as a direct impression upon his time-senses, so powerful as to overwhelm his other perceptions and to induce a kind of trance. In it he apprehended the complex of events which Sanfeil showed him as what is called a *gestalt* image, a whole impression made up from innumerable parts. It was, he said, like looking at a tapestry whose overall design one grasps at once although its details would take meticulous inspection to tease out.

It was not precisely like a tapestry, for it was solid. Indeed, it was more than solid, for it extended not only into those three spatial dimensions which are familiar to us all, but also into the fourth axis of temporal duration which only Lechasseur and his like are able to perceive. It did resemble a tapestry in being woven, although its constituents were not silk threads, but the threads of men's lives, the trails which Lechasseur refers to as the 'flesh-worms'. It was a static picture, for that which it represented was immutable, the unchanging shape of history itself; but its constituents appeared as if they were a seething mass of worm-bodies, frozen in a writhing frenzy.

These lives numbered, in total, many millions, and they intertwined in an intricate web which contrived to embody the whole condition of their little human society. From certain qualities of the tapestry's background (which underlay it as the cloth beneath the weft, and which he was, unfortunately, unable to describe in verbal terms), Lechasseur realised that he was being shown an image of his accustomed time and place, of Europe during the first half of the current century.

This much he understood immediately: examining this vision in greater detail, however, brought only perplexity, and numb awe at the overwhelming intricacy of each individual life, and all the more so at their myriad interwovennesses. The more closely he attempted to inspect the picture, the more complexity he found opening up before him: it was as if he were to view a forest, first from an aeroplane, then from a tall tower, then from the ground; and then to begin examining each tree-trunk through magnifying-glass and microscope. There was simply too great a proliferation of data for the human mind to absorb, and so Lechasseur's latched instead onto its broader, cruder trends. For had the image been a tapestry, he says, its pattern seen from a distance would have been clear and unambiguous.

Certain of the lives appeared to stand out from the others, thanks to a quality which Lechasseur would later describe in terms of pigment, for he 'saw' them as 'red', just as he had the traces of futurity which ran through Percival. The great majority of the flesh-worms were grey and undistinguished, but those of these few men glowed with a ruddy light like heated metal. The glowing lines proceeded unremarkably through the early part of the tapestry, until they were apparently altered by a particular event. Evidently this was of cataclysmic proportions, for like another, later band of darkness, its stain seeped through the whole cloth. Across its width, a band of time which corresponded to perhaps four or five years, countless of the un-luminous grey lives were cut off whole, their flesh-worms sliced apart in their millions, each terminating in a bloody, mangled form in one of Europe's innumerable muddy fields.

Beyond this catastrophe the life-shapes of the glowing men began to meet, in something like a complex mating-dance. Together they formed knots, connecting and corresponding and contriving, twisting apart and together like the vermiform feelers of a Coming Man's manipulating-hand. From their most concentrated ravellings emerged (usually at some remove) new lives, which glowed more brightly and more variously than they. These particoloured snake-threads of humanity spiralled gloriously through the world, culminating at last in a handful of multiply shining braids, which twisted suddenly into nothingness.

Allowing for its very different mode of expression, this information corresponded closely with what Emily and I had learned about the Hampdenshire Programme. The glowing flesh-worms were those of Gideon Beech's internationalists who had participated in the project and its analogues, while the polychromatic flesh-serpents were the shapes made by the lives of the supernormal children.

This tapestry of Lechasseur's, however, came with the benefit of Sanfeil's very deep historical perspective, and thus it also portrayed aspects of the future, as well as details from the past which were unknown to Beech. Lechasseur saw, for instance, that in the weaving of the supernormals' life-skeins the glowing men had drawn in, from all directions spatial and temporal, innumerable finer filaments of many 'colours'. These he supposed to represent ideas or objects rather than separate lives, suggesting that the ruddy men had incorporated material and techniques of diverse origins into their creations.

Then, too, when (having passed hastily across the second, darker apocalyptic region, which he had no desire to visit) he inspected that tangle of grey strands wherein the peculiar lives of the supernormals met their end, he saw that in its knot were also snagged two of the luminous ropes of the glowing men. These two emerged unharmed from the event which curtailed the existences of the supernormals (and whose spatial-temporal location Lechasseur now understands to have corresponded to the Retreat in June of 1950): he followed them to their own ends, which happened in succession some short while later.

He had at first surmised that the ruby glow of these life-worms had been an artificial marking, imposed upon the image by Sanfeil to demonstrate the significance of certain individuals to the overall scheme; but where these ruddy lives were cut off he now saw that they were made from two separate entities, the one containing the other as the insulation around an electric cable. In fact the outer, visible life was as grey and mundane as its neighbours; it was the inner life that glowed with the molten redness of futurity. These pallid flesh-worms had bloody parasites living within them; and these latter forms stretched away beyond those of their hosts, into the very dark and very distant future.

Each member of the Hampdenshire Programme, and certain others (as the three of us would realise later, when together we attempted to interpret this vision of Lechasseur's), had been under the influence of an observer from Sanfeil's own time.

Lechasseur found suddenly that his attention was being drawn against his will along one of those fiery trails, and once again he found himself precipitately hurled into the future, fetching up within the cavity where Percival, Sanfeil and he himself were sitting, long aeons after his accustomed era. Lechasseur's mind was reeling, and his bodily sensations told him that some time had passed: his stomach was empty, and his limbs were cramped. He flexed his muscles carefully.

Percival was coming round as well, and looked as stunned as Lechasseur himself; as well he might, after having had his question answered in such exhaustive detail. The young man made as if to speak, but there was a question which Lechasseur was impelled to put to Sanfeil first. 'Is that how you people see time?' he asked. 'The whole of history, laid out like that in front of you?'

'We do not,' Sanfeil said. 'Others have: men like yourself. There have been times in the grand history of man, Honoré, when entire cultures have shared your faculty of recognising time. It was their method of explication which I used.'

Percival could contain himself no longer, however. 'But how could they have understood – seeing it all like that, in so much detail? Surely they must have gone mad! There was so *much* of it, and so mixed-up, so confused. I couldn't make head nor tail of it, Sanfeil.'

Sanfeil's voice was as flat as ever. 'Honoré? What did you understand?'

Lechasseur looked from Sanfeil to Percival. 'I think,' he told the giant, 'that *your* people made *his* people. You bred them, back in the present, using people from our time as your ... well, "puppets" isn't quite right. I don't think you *made* anyone do it. You took something that was already there, and had it serve your purpose – whatever that is.'

'Oh, for God's sake!' Percival almost snarled. 'From all that marvellous, convoluted intricacy, you derive something so ... banal? Does all we saw just now amount in your mind to no more than *that*?'

'Mind you ...' – the boy was suddenly more thoughtful – '... I suppose that that *would* make for an interpretation, on the crudest level. Is it true, Sanfeil? Did you make my friends and me? Were you trying for people who could jump through time – am I one of your successes?'

'You are all successes, Percival,' Sanfeil said. 'The whole experiment has been a glorious success, and now it is at an end.'

'But if what Honoré says is right,' Percival said, 'then that would have to mean that my friends are going to die! Those soldiers will kill every one of us. How can we stop that from happening?'

Sanfeil seemed obscurely disappointed. 'Did you truly understand so little? I have said to you that all men die.'

'But you made us!' the young man insisted. 'Why would you abandon us to our deaths?'

Sanfeil explained: 'The experiment's purpose was to demonstrate that we in the future could retrospectively participate in our own origins, by influencing the development of our ancestors. This we have done, though not without impediments. Others have attempted to direct man's progress also, whether sojourners from another world or the distant descendants of my own generation, to whom my race of man is in its infancy. Such an influence we could not counteract. Yet still in you, Percival, and in the other specimens of your race, we saw the spirit of the cosmos express herself more vividly and fully than ever before on Earth. Your spirits burned more brightly than any before you.'

'Specimens!' Percival cried. 'Those are my people you're talking about! My friends!' He took himself in hand and, with that unnerving facility which I had observed in him on those other rare occasions when his passions were strong enough that they threatened to carry him away, he simply folded away his anger. Sensibly and quietly he asked: 'Surely you don't intend to destroy your own ancestors, Sanfeil? Look at everything we have in common – things which Honoré here couldn't begin to understand, any more than old Clever-clogs Erik.' (Lechasseur assures me that these were Percival's exact words.) 'It's perfectly obvious that mankind's future – his past, from your point of view – lies with us.'

'Your distress is quite understandable, Percival,' Sanfeil said. 'Naturally you are used to thinking of yourselves as the higher type, and Honoré's as the lower, and that is nothing but the truth. But you are wrong to believe that this means that you must live and they must die.'

'But the higher type must supersede the lower,' Percival said. 'It's nature's law.'

'In the long run, in the eye of history, that must always be true,' Sanfeil said. 'You are our glorious precursors, an early leitmotif anticipating our great crescendo. You are anachronisms.'

'But you can't let us die,' Percival insisted levelly. 'If we die in the past, then you in your present will cease to exist.'

The green man said, 'But you are not our ancestors, Percival. Honoré's people are.'

Percival paled. 'What?' he cried.

Finding himself unequal to the temptation, Lechasseur interjected, 'I have to say I worked that one out a couple of minutes ago.'

Sanfeil continued, 'You say, if your race dies, that my people can never come to be. On the contrary, it is the extinction of your people that gives life to mine. This must happen, Percival, and neither you nor I nor any other may prevent it. Before it can burn brighter, your light must become diffused throughout the whole race of mankind. Your lives will be ploughed back into the Earth, that she may bring forth more abundant life. It is your life-energy, that spark expressed in you so brilliantly and briefly, that shall impel the rest of humankind on that long and painful evolutionary ascent, and at last to the glory which you see around you now. It is they, not you, who are to be the Coming Men.'

'This will be an atrocity,' said Percival. 'To let creatures like us die, so that creatures like *him* may live? We are the higher type – we will not be subsumed into the lower! It goes against every principle we have.'

'On the contrary,' said Sanfeil. 'It conforms with your highest principle, as you yourself would see if your mind was not occluded still by the subhuman within you. You must allow your own brief efflorescence to fade, so that I and my kind may come into being. We are more fully human than you: in us the Spirit of Man waxes greater and nobler than ever before. Far more so than in your little race.

'My people are the more developed type, and your deaths will enable that development. It will be a noble sacrifice, Percival, to allow your kind to pass in order that a better may arise.'

1. THE THING HAPPENS

The night which followed my arrival I spent in a single room of one of the Retreat's outbuildings. The children slept communally, as they performed most of their daily tasks, but they kept some rooms apart in a converted stables for those rare occasions when the need for privacy might arise.

Emily and I had conversed late with Beech, Violet and the others. We three visitors had at the playwright's insistence been conducted around the machine-shed where the residents kept the majority of their marvellous inventions. Ever the dilettante, Beech had asked wearyingly many technical questions relating to the frequency of psychic wave-lengths and the like, before consenting to retire. The three of us had been allocated neighbouring rooms, and the children left us there. A watch had been assigned to the perimeter, in case the 'soldier gang' attempted any infiltration. Violet and another girl were to take the first shift.

I did not sleep. My renewed contact with these exceptional young people, together with the other frantic occurrences of the past days, conspired efficiently to sabotage my repose: additionally, I had been unsettled to a great degree by the facts which Gideon Beech had disclosed.

At four o'clock in the morning, I was disturbed by a bold knock at my bedroom door. I rose, my heart percussing painfully, and called,

'Please wait a moment.' Opening the door I discovered Emily, fully dressed, although the state of her clothes implied that she had been endeavouring to sleep in them. Apologising for my own night-attire, I bade her enter.

Emily, who as I have mentioned was in her outlook a most unconventional young woman, sat down on my bed. 'I hoped you'd be awake,' she said. 'Mr Beech got up an hour or so ago, I think. I haven't heard him come back.' I remarked that old men rarely slept well, as I had cause to appreciate. She made a rueful face, and said that some young women had trouble also.

Despite the season, the night air on the hillside was chill, and the Retreat's inhabitants, whose constitutions were sturdier than ours, seemed not to be greatly concerned with the heating of their accommodation. I drew my dressing-gown about me tightly, and joined Emily on the bed. 'Erik, how long have you known these children?' she asked me.

I considered the question carefully. 'In Percival's case, nearly ten years,' I said. 'The others rather less: as you will recall, you made Violet's acquaintance before I did. Why do you ask?'

'It's just that they seem so trusting of you,' Emily said. 'And not only you, but Mr Beech and me as well. Given that they're planning to wipe us all out, it seems rather rash of them, don't you think? How do they know I'm not in league with these soldiers?'

'Well, they are telepathic,' I said reasonably. 'As for wiping us out, I don't honestly believe that they plan anything of the kind. It seems to me that all their rhetoric on the subject is philosophical rather than pragmatic. It is a point of faith with them that their species will overtake our own, and I believe that evolutionary precedent is on their side in the matter. They have no reason to attempt to hasten the process, although they will naturally defend themselves if they are threatened.'

'Well, if you're that fatalistic about it then they've nothing to fear from you,' Emily declared. 'And Mr Beech is obviously keen to be associated with the winning side. Which leaves me ... and it occurs to me that bringing me here is a much better way of keeping me under control than leaving me in London, knowing what I know.'

'Oh, come now,' I began to say, but I was interrupted. An oppressive sense of panic, without apparent cause or antecedent, settled upon me like heavy earth in a grave. Cries of alarm began to arise from outside the building, accompanied after a moment or two by the sound of booted, running feet. 'Good heavens!' I exclaimed in confusion. 'Whatever is going on?'

'It's the attack,' Emily said, and my appalled senses became aware that a sharp stuttering which occasionally overlaid the cacophony outside could only be the noise of gunfire. 'We have to leave at once.'

'But no-one can attack the Retreat,' I stupidly asserted. 'The defences –'

'Never mind that!' cried Emily. 'They may not have found the car yet.' Opening the door, she quickly checked the corridor outside for intruders, then beckoned me ahead. I shivered in my flimsy coverings as I succeeded her out of the building and into the night. A number of the indoor lights had been switched on, throwing a dozen squares of yellow onto the muddy grass. Silhouettes of running men and shafts of light from torches were everywhere. Almost immediately a man was upon us, and I panicked; but Emily's limbs moved quickly in the dark, and a moment later our assailant lay groaning on the muddy ground.

Emily led me grimly onward through the mayhem, and I quickly lost all sense of our location. We had travelled perhaps forty paces before we were pinioned in the intersecting beams of a pair of torches, and a rough voice called out, 'Stop right there!' I was dazzled, but could nonetheless detect, within the circles of illumination, the tips of gun-barrels trained upon us. I endeavoured to follow Emily's example by raising my hands, but my limbs would not co-operate. I was shaking like a sapling, although whether from the cold or from the shock of finding myself once again upon a battlefield as I, a young medical orderly, had been so long ago in France, I have no clear notion.

'It's the damned normals,' a second voice offered, and one of the gun-barrels was lowered.

Coarsely, the first said: 'You mean the _____ traitors.' The accent was unmistakeably American.

'Save it for later, Krovsky,' said the other. By contrast this man's voice was that of a working-class Londoner, and I would shortly learn that

Emily knew him as 'PC Grayles,' the constable who had questioned her at St Pancras Station. 'The Colonel don't want these ones damaged,' said Grayles. 'Just get them out of the way.' Muscular fingers gripped Emily's and my shoulders, and we were forcibly marched into the farmhouse, where Gideon Beech, composed and fully dressed, sat waiting for us in the kitchen.

'These the ones?' the American named Krovsky asked Beech. The light of the kitchen exhibited our captor to my scrutiny, and I saw that he was the same man who had been St John Spears' chauffeur. Now that I came to examine him more closely he was of a particular Slavic type, stocky, brutal and intractable. As a fighting-man, I thought, he would be cruel, and difficult to hurt. He had a visor covering his face which I though at first must be a gas-mask, but it concealed neither mouth nor nose: circles of dark glass shielded the eyes, however, and a pair of elaborate box-like constructions enclosed the ears. The man's kit bore no identifying insignia, and would have been more accurately classed as combat fatigues than as a uniform.

Beech said, 'Please sit down, Miss Blandish – you too, Clevedon. This shouldn't take too long. I trust you've not been hurt?' Still shivering, I moved closer to the stove, which had been recently lit, and seated myself there.

'Is this your doing, Mr Beech?' asked Emily coldly. Beech conceded that, regrettably but necessarily, it was. 'In that case I'd prefer to stand,' she replied.

Krovsky pushed her roughly down into a chair. 'Stay put,' he said. He left us, slamming the door and locking us inside with Gideon Beech.

2. MORE OPINIONS OF BEECH

It would be some while before Emily and I were able to piece together the whole story of the assault upon the Retreat. At the time we were most certainly not inclined to inquire of Beech precisely what actions he had taken in order to lay the farmstead open to the soldiers, although Emily's initial supposition that he had contrived somehow to disable the psychic amplification machine upon which the automatic defences relied would prove to have been well founded.

For the attack to have been mounted at all must certainly have taken a considerable use of resources on St John Spears' part; but it was obvious by now that such were at his disposal. The operation could scarcely have occurred, even in such an insignificant region of the British Isles, without the blessing of His Majesty's Government; and whatever other lies he might have told me, it would transpire that Mr Spears really was a millionaire.

As later conversations would establish, Beech had been approached by Spears on the afternoon which followed my own rejection of the pretended philanthropist's advances. The American's visit to me had been nearly his last resort in attempting to locate the supernormals' sanctuary: it was only by coincidence that one of his staff had intercepted a telegram from Percival in London to Gideon Beech, and Spears had held out little hope that one of Beech's known evolutionary opinions would be sympathetic to his goals.

That evening Beech had awaited the imminent arrival of his young friend Jelena, and had obediently allowed her to remove him to the Retreat, whose location he had earlier surrendered to Spears without demur. With us and with the children he had conferred in detail upon their plans for the farm's defence, and he had paid meticulous attention as they conducted us around their assorted miraculous machines. Rising at three when he considered that Emily and I would likely be asleep (he was mistaken, but in the event neither of us suspected him sufficiently to challenge him), he had sabotaged the psychical amplifier, and had then signalled to a soldier on a nearby hilltop using nothing more sophisticated than Morse code and a hand-torch.

The waiting soldiers breached the perimeter without harm, and with Beech's information were able quickly to find and to dispatch the sentries ('Argos' of the many eyes was on duty at the time, with a youth named Lucas). Each of the individual supernormals would have been able to mount a psychical assault against a single soldier which would have been painful at the very least; but just as the simple head-sets worn by Grayles and his colleague at St Pancras had protected them against Violet's evasions, so the bulkier models which had been issued to the attackers formed a potent barrier against any such offensive. Additionally, a former stage-magician whom Spears had bizarrely recruited to his employ had placed the men in a mild hypnotic trance, which supposedly acted as a further safeguard against psychic infiltration.

The Retreat fell to the invaders within the space of an hour. It was possible that there might have been other devices in the machine-workshop which could have aided the defenders; indeed, Jimmie had been observed in that very place, apparently attempting frantically to activate one of them. The young mechanical genius had subsequently vanished, which (though they were keeping the machine-shed well guarded) was a matter of serious concern to Spears and his men.

For the moment, however, we knew little of this. Our greatest preoccupation (or rather Emily's, since if I am honest my own primary concern was to warm myself up sufficiently to avoid hypothermia) was to establish why it was that Beech had betrayed our supernormal friends.

'The children trusted you,' said Emily quietly. 'How could you set those soldiers on them?'

The old man said: 'I presume that you intend the question morally, Miss Blandish, but it has a practical application also. How could I possibly betray the young people when they trusted me? How was I able, in other words, to conceal my intent from them? And for that matter, how was I able to incapacitate their arcane devices?'

'That isn't what I meant,' said Emily; but I could see that Beech had aroused her interest.

'Then perhaps it is what you should have meant,' the playwright said. 'If this little operation fails, then it's a skill which we may all have to learn to cultivate. Let these young people only live, and in a few years' time the rest of us will be their slaves at best. You've heard them talk: their very existence makes us obsolete, they say; and that's a thing I've no desire to be.

'I will admit that winning this trust of theirs (which I have, incidentally, no regrets about betraying) has been a long and arduous struggle. It has required enormous, and if I did not wish to be scrupulously accurate I might say superhuman, self-discipline and control, together with some advanced auto-mesmeric technique which I have picked up at no small personal expense. Fortunately, the children are secure enough in their own superiority that they are bound to underestimate a cuckoo in their midst. Not that they are wrong, for the most part, to be so: I would not wish you to think that. Each of them is by far superior to the average *Homo sapiens* man or woman. There are, however, a few of us among the parent species (statistical monsters, genii) who are so far *above* the average that we may rival, and even in some respects may better, these youthful specimens of the peculiar; particularly when we have ourselves attained a sagacious maturity.

'It is we few, we precious few in all the meanings of that hackneyed scribblers' phrase, who now stand like a bastion between the venerable race of mankind and his enslavement or extinction ...'

Thus, and much more, spoke Gideon Beech. Yet while he had been speaking I had formed the impression, which quickly became a firm conviction, that in actuality the old man had very little idea of how he had been able to deceive the supernormals; and that, if he had not been able to fall comfortably back upon his monumental personal conceit, he would have been at a loss to account for it.

When I had first read one of Beech's plays, nearly a half-century earlier, I had felt myself inspired by the nobility of its author's ambition. I had been already cognisant despite my relative youth that any devotion I might feel to family, class, country or any other of the phantom causes to which a man is popularly invited to pledge his loyalties, would constitute nothing more worthy than a mean-spirited and partial extension of my own self-interest. The work of Beech identified, espoused and bruited forth a greater allegiance: a wider patriotism which adopted mankind, indeed the whole of life itself, as its constituency. This cause, I knew at once, must override every one of the meagre obsessions of which I was expected to partake. I felt the spirit of his words call out to me, awakening within me a yearning to raise mankind beyond his current limits, to shape him into a more complete expression of his lofty potential.

Well, I had been substantially correct. The soul in Beech which had cried out to me (or rather to that spirit in me which Sanfeil strove always to awaken), was not Beech's own, but that of his own far-future observer and controller.

3. THE STORY OF SPEARS

It is the same boundless self-confidence which causes the American male to be so admirable and attractive in defeat, which renders him all but insufferable in victory. So it was with Mr (or, as it seemed I now must call him, Colonel) St John Spears, when some time later he, along with Grayles, deigned to pay the three of us a visit in the farmhouse kitchen. Like his men, Spears wore black overalls lacking insignia, but there was no doubt from the deferential stance and mode of address which all adopted when he was present, that he was the commander of their renegade force. Though evidently fatigued, as were we all, he bore with him an air of self-satisfaction which suggested that he considered the capture of the Retreat to be no small achievement for himself, and perhaps also (as I perceived it, and no doubt my judgement was impaired by my dislike of the man) as no small triumph over me personally.

Despite this, I confess that my first reaction upon seeing him was one of pathetic gratitude, for he had brought the suit-case containing my clothing from my bedroom in the stables, and I was permitted five minutes in which to go upstairs with the flat-eyed Grayles and dress myself. As I did so, it occurred to me that the two men had only removed their protective head-pieces once they had come inside the house. I wondered whether this implied merely that Spears was taking no chances, or that some of the Retreat's rightful inhabitants had eluded their custody. Not being aware of Jimmie's abscondment, however, I concluded that they were probably concerned about the missing Percival.

I might have been cold, scared and profoundly exhausted, but this had not eclipsed my fellow-feeling for the children, who I was certain must be worse off in their captivity than I. When I returned downstairs, I gathered that Emily had been haranguing Spears on this very point. 'For now, Miss Blandish, all we're doing is keeping them under control,' he said. 'We still have plans for them – I should say our partners do. We had to pull in ten kinds of favour from your government to be here at all, and Mr Beech's scientific friends had some requests as well. The kids are safe for now, though, you have my word.'

'Safe "for now"?' Emily repeated. 'You must forgive me, Colonel, if I don't feel your word's worth much when you qualify it like that. What conditions are you holding them under, please? If it comes to that, what *laws* are you holding them under?'

Spears sighed. 'We're here with the authority of the British government, so you'll forgive *me* if I'm disposed to let them handle the legal niceties. As for conditions – most of them are in their meeting-room, under armed guard. We've taken steps to neutralise their telepathic assault capabilities. Other than that we're being as humane as we can – more than we have to be, take it from me.'

Further enquiries disclosed that the supernormal children had been fitted (forcibly, in many cases) with head-sets of their own. These were not the same type with which the soldiers had been issued, but simpler devices for generating noise of a loud, random and distracting nature: they were carefully designed to prohibit the wearer from exercising mental concentration in any degree, and would therefore, it was hoped, prevent the children from utilising their psychical abilities. To stop them from removing the machines, each of the children had been handcuffed to one of the chairs in the meeting-chamber. To me, as it is probably unnecessary to remark, this seemed a brutally barbaric way to treat a fellow human being, let alone a child, but to Spears it was an elementary precaution.

Emily asked after Violet in particular. I suppose that, just as I felt a particular bond towards Percival, so she felt protective towards the young urchin who had first drawn her into all this mess. Spears was reluctant to reply, but Emily was a persuasive, forthright young person, and the Colonel eventually revealed that Violet was being kept separately from the others. 'She's of interest to Mr Beech's biologist friends, that's all. They want to know more about her condition.'

'Her condition? Is Violet ill?' Emily stared at Spears. 'You surely don't mean she's pregnant?'

'So we understand, Miss Blandish. The information came from Mr Beech.'

'Is this true, Beech?' I asked. 'I understood that none of them had yet managed to conceive.'

'"No viable offspring" is I think the way they usually put it,' Beech mused. 'Who knows if this child would have been the one to break that run of luck?'

Emily, who was more concerned about Violet's current circumstances than her child's prospects, challenged Spears fiercely as to the morality of applying what she called 'psychological torture' to a lame and pregnant girl; but the Colonel was intractable. A short while later he left us, locking the three of us in once more.

As I would discover when I came to investigate the Colonel's personal history, he had good reason to be cautious of the supernormals' mental powers. Some of his story I obtained, reluctantly on both our parts, from Beech once the crisis was over, while other particulars came to me from certain of the political contacts whom I have made over the years (and who have not yet deserted me quite to a man).

St John Spears was born the heir to a prosperous Boston manufacturing family, but one whose paterfamilias believed in 'toughening up' his sons to prepare them for what he called the 'cut and thrust' of business life. At his father's insistence, young St John had joined the Army shortly before the entry of the United States into the last war, and had distinguished himself by his great bravery on behalf of the men in his care. (He had, we discovered, been briefly billeted at the same small town in Northern France as Lechasseur, but neither man had any cause to remember the other.) In the late stages of the war

Spears had been co-opted by the commanders of the Allies, given the precocious rank of Colonel, and set to leading a highly secret task-force which was intended to accompany the final Allied assault on Germany.

Throughout the war there had been rumours on both sides of German 'miracle weapons', created at the behest of the Führer himself, which would, it was asserted, result in uncontested victory once deployed. The consensus on the Allied side was that such stories were mostly propaganda (especially since by this time the Germans were conspicuously getting the worst of the conflict), but it was known that there had been actual programmes of research into extraordinary weapons: the V-1 bomb and V-2 rocket had been the macabre fruits of just such a project. Spears' international team was charged with locating all such weaponry and capturing or, failing that, dismantling it.

In this goal, insofar as I can ascertain through layers of bureaucratic and military obfuscation, they enjoyed considerable success. After the German defeat, Spears testified to his opinion that potentially dangerous remains could still exist throughout Germany and the states which she had occupied. As a consequence of some political manoeuvring which I confess remains obscure to me, authority over his command passed from the Allies to the United Nations, and the unit ceased to be strictly military by formal definition, for all it remained so effectively. Spears was given leave to continue with his mission throughout the nations of Europe, including all four of the German occupation zones.

It is, naturally enough, extremely difficult to find out exactly which types of weapon Spears' men were compelled to decommission during this time; and, such information not being germane to the matter in hand, I have not attempted to do so. What I have learned is that Spears began in late 1947 to encounter rumours of one particular programme of research, whose materials had not merely been left idle after the war but which was supposedly being prosecuted still, in secret and with funding from certain senior surviving members of the National Socialist party. The research supposedly involved *lebenwaffen*, 'weapons that lived', and it was Spears' conjecture that this phrase referred to some form of artificial biological plague.

Spears' investigations led him to Upper Bavaria, to a small mountain village where a private clinic run by one Dr Mannheim, late of the University of Ingolstadt, had remained open since the war despite a lack of obvious business. The clinic proved to be heavily guarded, and Spears' men found themselves, for the first time since the conclusion of the official hostilities, embroiled in actual combat. Mannheim's security guards defended the building fiercely, and the doctor himself was captured only after he had destroyed every one of his notes.

While attempting to consolidate his control of the complex, Spears discovered that the clinic contained a sealed inner compound. The captive Mannheim killed himself before he could be questioned concerning its contents.

Convinced now that he had uncovered a very dangerous plot against Germany's erstwhile enemies, Spears called on the aid of the United States' occupying forces in the region. Immunological experts were summoned from England and France, and stood by along with American soldiers as Spears' men opened up the inner compound of the clinic. Out through the open doors stepped seven children, each between four and eight years old, and wearing crisp starched uniforms of the Hitler Youth. Each of them held a hand-grenade, and the foremost of them, a muscular blond lad with a serious, intelligent face, told them in flawless English that his brothers, his sisters and he would die before being taken by the foes of the Reich.

This proved to be a feint. As the Americans began a hasty evacuation of all but a few negotiators, the children launched against the retreating men a psychical attack which, drawing corporately upon the siblings' combined power, was several orders of magnitude more potent than that which Percival would unleash against Lechasseur two years later. Most of the soldiers and attendant experts collapsed, some of them undergoing spasms and haemorrhages. A handful, Spears among them, found themselves irrationally overtaken by blind animal panic, trampled their colleagues in their rush to quit the clinic, and ran and ran until exhaustion claimed them. Those who fled were the survivors: inside the compound, the supernormal children calmly primed their hand-grenades, positioned them amongst the incapacitated men, and made off into the mountains together.

Two weeks later in a psychiatric hospital in Munich, Colonel Spears recovered from a deep fugue, to discover that nine-tenths of his troops were dead, or had suffered irreparable damage to their bodies and minds. Bathetically, he also learned that he was now the owner of the family business, his father having died of a heart attack on being told of his son's condition.

As soon as he was able to quit the hospital, Spears contacted the United Nations to resign his commission, and returned to America, where against the protests of the family he liquidated his business assets in their entirety. He then assembled those remnants of his task-force who still had the stomach for the job, and armed them for war.

Dr Mannheim's brood of infant supermen had dispersed, scattering as best they could across the globe. Some of them had hidden themselves away in distant places, while some had sought refuge with the progeny of the Hampdenshire Project and its equivalents. Over the past two years, Spears' unit (now operating without the authority of the UN or that of any government, although they found that there was covert support for what they did in every country where supernormals had inadvertently been bred) had worked tirelessly to hunt down, harry and destroy the Mannheim children, and all the other communities of *Homo peculiar* where they had found succour.

Six of those children were already dead when Spears visited me at my house in London. The last of them remaining was little blue-eyed Freia.

4. A PERSONAL REVELATION

And now I must, I fear, divulge a matter which I was not able to explain to Emily then or later, and which I may feel sanguine enough to mention now purely because of my certain knowledge that the present volume will form my final literary communication with the world.

Like Emily, I had been much distressed by Spears' news of Violet's state of health, and of her captivity. I was, of course, equally unhappy at the thought of Mary, Freia and the others forced to endure handcuffing and the deprivation of their mental powers; although I found that I was thankful that at least Percival, my own particular protégé, was not among them. But this relief was dashed by the information, awkwardly imparted by Spears before he left us once again, that three of the children were already killed. They were the sentries Lukas and 'Argos', and the lovely Jelena, who had succeeded in relieving a soldier of his gun and had maimed several of his comrades, before Krovsky had taken a grenade and blown her up along with a considerable part of one of the outbuildings.

The situation was dreadful, whichever way one looked at it. From one point of view, these children, far from innocent perhaps, but very probably the greatest hope mankind had for the future, were being tormented and slain. From the other point of view, espoused by Beech and Spears, this necessary slaughter was occasioned by the stated determination of one small group of deviants to commit an atrocious act of genocide whose parallel had never been witnessed in the human race's history. To the most uninformed observer, the moral aims of both the parties, once explained, would have been repugnant in the extreme.

To Emily Blandish, a woman with a strong and passionate sense of justice, such a state of affairs required some assignation of responsibility. This is not to say that she was a moraliser by habit, or vindictive by nature. I am quite certain that, had the two of us been free to act or even to contact the outside world, she would have done everything possible to aid her young friend, and her friend's friends. But every means of egress from the cottage was either locked or barred, we were one physically slight young woman and an old man, and we had seen when the door had been opened that one of the soldiers stood guard outside. We were moreover constantly under the eye of another who, somewhat ambivalent though his current status might appear, had amply demonstrated by his actions his support for our captors and their goal. Under these circumstances, Emily's natural rage at the abuse of our young friends had no other recourse than that of finding someone whom she might blame.

There was no shortage of candidates. Beech, as he willingly admitted, had betrayed the supernormals and allowed the soldiers to overrun the Retreat. Colonel Spears had ordered that Violet and the other children should be incarcerated; his men had shown, at the very least, a culpable moral negligence in unquestioningly following his commands. In some respects, guiltless though she undoubtedly was, I am sure that Emily even held herself accountable for the catastrophe: perhaps for allowing Violet to return to the Retreat, or for failing to challenge Beech earlier.

The one interested party whom Emily apparently did not blame for the disaster was me; and yet it seemed to me, as I sat listening to her furiously arguing principles with the old man, that in this, if in little else, she was entirely mistaken.

For I knew that the present sorry circumstances resulted directly from the Hampdenshire Project and its cousins. Without their fateful interference, Percival and all the others would have been ordinary children: undistinguished, dull, perhaps even stupid; but free from persecution, innocent of murderous intent, never required to shoulder the terrible responsibilities which accompanied their actual superhuman state. Without the eugenical programmes, there would have been no question of older humanity's being brushed aside in the service of a greater end, nor of the premature cessation of all these young lives. Spears would have been an industrial capitalist, neither more nor less harmful than many others; Beech would have been a reclusive old man; Lechasseur and Percival would not be lost, and Emily and I would not be prisoners.

I had not been, as Beech claimed that he had, one of the masterminds behind the Hampdenshire conspiracy, nor even one of its ordinary members (if you have supposed that I was, then I am afraid I must disappoint you). Unlike the other actors of my generation in this story (Beech, my old friend Dr Tremaine, even the Bavarian doctor, Mannheim), I had never even been aware of the project's existence.

And yet with all of these men I had made common cause.

My lectures, my novels, my books of philosophy: in all of them I had enthusiastically propounded the exact ideas on which the project, and its German analogue, had been based. I had written extensively and evangelically upon the subjects of eugenics and of sociological planning. I had not done so idly or without thought for the moral consequences, nor even with the intellectual detachment which one might expect of a philosopher; but zealously, with passion and the firm intention of bringing as many of my peers as I might around to my opinions.

I had insisted that mankind must take himself in hand and build himself anew: a better race of human being, I had assured my readers, was the only goal that was worth pursuing, the only goal which might in time bring all our other noble aspirations within the scope of our achievement. Those of us who were capable of seeing clearly (among whom, naturally, I accounted myself and all the others who had been inspired by the aloof idealism of such thinkers as Beech and Mr Wells: all those of us whom the old playwright had carelessly and proprietorially claimed as his internationalists) must guide, cajole and, if necessary, coerce the masses who refused to see matters as we did.

Had Tremaine told me of his involvement in the Hampdenshire

Programme (as, to tell the truth, I am still hurt that he did not), I would have applauded it whole-heartedly, praised its high ideals, begged to be allowed to be involved.

It may seem strange that this realisation came as a moral revelation to me. I had long known, after all, that Percival considered his species to be in competition with my own. I knew that when the crisis came it would involve no small deal of suffering for all. In theory I believed that, for the human spirit to prevail, the higher type of men might have to eliminate the lower altogether, and that this would entail the death of all I knew: my friends, my family, my country, and what was more sacred to me than any of these, the spiritual and the aesthetic values which *Homo sapiens* has struggled to establish for himself.

I told myself that I should rejoice in such a sacrifice; that I should revel in it, as in the sombre passage of a symphony which by its contrast renders the later movements all the gayer. I knew that this was how Percival himself should feel were our roles reversed and, perverse though it may have seemed to draw my spiritual understanding from a young boy, I believed that in this matter his insight was profound.

Yet I had always held out a small hope that *Homo sapiens* might improve himself still; that the grandchildren of my generation might yet scramble upright, and stand as equals with Percival and his kin; that, given sufficient impetus, the two species of men (assuming that they did not indeed become identical through interbreeding) might build a utopian future together.

Percival had always known that this was a futile hope; and so, perhaps, had I.

It is one thing to contemplate in serene equanimity the sacrifice of oneself and all that one loves. It is another matter altogether to be forced to watch while the same thing happens to others. My spiritual conviction still insisted that whatever occurred would serve the purposes of what I am afraid I still think of at times by the old, discredited name of 'God'; yet at the knowledge of it my humanity rose up within me and cried out, 'No more!'

I realised, blinking through my tears, that Emily had noticed my distress. I would, I sincerely believe, have explained to her my feelings, even though it meant admitting my complicity in all the horror that surrounded us. I would have done so, if for no other reason then merely to avoid her reaching the otherwise inevitable conclusion that I was weeping from terror for my own life.

However, I cannot be certain even of this, for I was not permitted the luxury of opportunity for such a confession. Quite suddenly and shockingly, as the three of us sat there in the kitchen, inwardly mortified, angry or smug according to our respective natures, there was a crackling noise, a flash like lightning; and we each turned to behold the sweat-slicked, breathless faces of Honoré Lechasseur and Percival.

1. A PHILOSOPHICAL ISSUE

Our reactions to this unexpected apparition were several. Gideon Beech, who knew Percival but was unaware of the phenomenon of time-channelling, gaped and spluttered. I exclaimed something idiotic like 'My God – Percival! Thank Heavens you're safe! And I suppose this must be Mr Lechasseur.'

The smile which Emily gave to her friend spoke of her very sincere relief at seeing him safe and well, but her first words were: 'Honoré, there are armed soldiers holding these poor children prisoner. We have to help them.'

'Wait just a moment,' Percival said. 'It's no use our going off at half-cock.' From the authority in his voice I would never have believed that Lechasseur had seen him so recently in such a wretched state. Seating himself gratefully on one of the hard kitchen chairs, he continued: 'We've had a very long journey (thank Heaven we had the light of your inner genius to guide us here, Clever-clogs), and there's an awful lot at stake – maybe the survival of both our species. You'd better bring us up to speed before we do anything else.'

Such was his calmness of manner that we all acceded to his request. Emily and I sat down once more, and were joined by Lechasseur. Beech had not moved, and was unable to disguise his apprehension. He looked his age for the first time since he and I had met.

A few minutes sufficed for us to explain most of what had occurred, beginning with the matter of Beech's betrayal ('Well, never mind that now,' Percival said lightly), and continuing with the fall of the Retreat, the incarceration of the supernormals, and Spears' special interest in Violet. Emily also gave a concise summary of the small-arms carried by the soldiers, which I had not had the presence of mind to have observed in any detail. Percival listened intently, his expression becoming grimmer by increments. When we had finished he asked us a few pertinent questions relating to what little Spears had told us of the history of the assault, and of the conditions of the children's imprisonment. Then he said, 'Our first job has to be breaking ourselves out of here.'

From this point onward, incidents progressed with a rapidity which would shortly become bewildering to me. The zeal with which Percival had returned from the future was intense, and the facility with which he took command of the events and lives at the Retreat was really quite alarming.

In service of his first objective, Percival immediately commenced battering at the hinges of the farmhouse door with one of the heavy chairs. Our guard, believing that the room held only two frail men and a recalcitrant young woman, came in to admonish us: he stopped dead at the sight of Lechasseur (Beech cried, 'Look out, fool!', but too late), and Percival knocked the soldier senseless with the chair.

Our young friend spent a moment or two in studying the fallen man's head-piece, then nodded in satisfaction. Releasing the buckles on the device and lifting it from the slack face, he told us, 'Now for Violet,' and led us out onto the hillside, into the streaming morning light.

Before we followed the young man, Lechasseur made a brief examination of our erstwhile guard, concluding, 'He's alive.' The American sounded as surprised as I: I well recalled certain discussions with Percival, during the phase of his adolescence when his emerging philosophy had made some talk upon the morality of killing others more than imperative. In the end, to my discomfiture, I had had to agree that we should differ on the matter.

The four of us followed cautiously in Percival's wake, but apart from a few distant soldiers patrolling the perimeter there seemed to be nobody about. The insensible guard we locked inside the farmhouse with his own keys. Lechasseur strode ahead to join Percival, while Emily and I held back to keep a close watch on Beech, who the American had insisted should accompany us despite my own reservations on the matter.

Our friends made for one of the outbuildings, where another soldier stood on guard. He failed to observe their approach, and between them they were able quickly to incapacitate him. I saw Percival leap on to the man's back like a tiger, stuffing a fist into his mouth to prevent him from raising the alarm, while Lechasseur felled him with a blow to the head. The Negro would later admit that, after the burdensome gravity of Sanfeil's time, his body felt 'airy, as if I was made of cotton wool'. He had no trouble in operating physically, despite the exertion of his recent arduous time-journey: instead, he felt light-headed and mildly delirious.

From the recumbent guard Percival took the head-set and a bunch of keys, with which he opened up the building and vanished inside. Lechasseur carried the fallen man indoors, and the rest of us followed. By the time we had caught up with Percival, the lad had released Violet both from her shackles and from the shrieking ear-pieces which Spears' men had forced on her, and whose workings were now spread across the floor.

'Freia's in one of the store-rooms,' Violet said as soon as she saw us, and at the same moment Percival tossed the keys to Lechasseur. The American and Emily set off to find the German girl, leaving Beech and me alone with the two young people.

They were staring at one another, silently and intently. It was clear that they were involved in telepathic communication at a profound level.

After some moments their silence began to make me feel uneasy, and I felt that I could hardly strike up a conversation with Beech. 'You're turning things around awfully quickly,' I observed to Percival. After our many hours interned immobile in the kitchen at the cottage, I felt genuinely befuddled by the succession of fights and escapes which had filled the past few minutes. It had indeed occurred to me to wonder whether I might not have inadvertently fallen asleep beside the warm stove.

My friend's engrossed expression did not alter appreciably as he answered: 'Of course I am, Clever-clogs. I'm "strangely gifted", remember?'

'But after all,' I said, 'you're only one supernormal. Your friends have been here all this while. Why haven't they done anything equally inspired?'

'Well,' Percival said, 'we don't know for sure that they haven't. I'd imagine not, though.' Violet nodded suddenly at him, and broke into a charming smile, as my young friend turned his intent eyes toward me.

'Actually,' he said, 'it's the very thing that I've just been explaining to Violet. It's a philosophical issue really, as you of all people should have supposed. That principle you've heard me expound so many times – that evolution's will must needs be done, and that the higher type must prevail over the lower – tends to breed a certain fatalism. You get to thinking that, if someone *can* get the better of you, that means that they *should*. For now, the others (excepting Vi) still believe in that, but I've grown beyond it. Don't worry, I'll soon set them right.'

Despite the fact that I had recently arrived at similar conclusions myself, I felt obscurely disappointed. 'I had supposed you wedded to that principle,' I said, 'for good or ill.'

'In sickness and in health, eh?' He grinned. 'Well, so had I. That was before I met people who really were, and saw what it had made of them. I've changed my mind on a number of points, Clever-sticks, the first of them being that old notion of mine that only one or the other of our species can emerge from a crisis like this intact. And on that matter, old man, there's something I need to tell you.'

An awful apprehension gripped me suddenly, but before I could respond little Freia arrived, with Lechasseur and Emily, her arms angrily crossed. Believing the children of the Mannheim project to be the most dangerous of the supernormals, Spears had ordered that the German girl be kept apart from the others with a guard to herself, and this man Lechasseur had once again been obliged to incapacitate.

Freia appeared surprisingly little affected by her experiences. This had not, of course, been the first time in her short life when adversity had sent forth arms and fighting-men to seek her out. She handed her still-screeching ear-pieces to Percival, and said, 'You and Honoré must have come a very long way, Percival. Your shapes are stretched out *extremely* thinly.'

As Violet took the child aside, Emily said indignantly to Percival: 'Freia tells me you have some kind of doomsday weapon, here at the Retreat. And that it's primed and ready to be let off.'

'Ah yes,' said Percival. 'I was just about to talk to Erik about that. We don't have much time to address the matter, though,' he said, 'so please try not to fly off the handle when I tell you about it.'

2. THE TERMINAL

We listened in appalled fascination as Percival explained to us the function and the purpose of 'the terminal': a function and a purpose quite in keeping with the philosophy upon which the Retreat had been founded. As Percival described it, the terminal was quite simply a weapon of unprecedented apocalyptic power, designed with one sole end in mind, which was the extinction of *Homo sapiens*.

When active, the terminal would generate a psychic 'wave-form', carefully chosen so as to be susceptible to propagation through the medium of the Earth itself. This wave would resonate with certain characteristic vibrations in the normal human brain, and would do so with such catastrophic violence as to strip the contents of that brain clean away. Across the globe, mankind (always excepting the supernormals, whose brains vibrated at much higher frequencies) would lose all power of speech, of understanding, of perception and even of independent movement. Those members of the species who did not expire instantly from shock would starve within a week, blind, incontinent and mindless.

'I don't mean any of you chaps, of course,' Percival added hastily. 'We can use our own minds to protect the few of you, if it should come to it. That's the theory, at least: of course we haven't tried it out. Now please,' he protested, 'didn't I ask you not to make a song and dance of this? It won't come to that if we can help it.

'The trouble is … well, Jimmie got a general telepathic message out just before he disappeared, saying that he'd managed to get the dratted machine all ready to go. It wasn't really finished, but Jimmie's dashed clever. He evidently managed to lash it up somehow.'

The instant that anybody lacking the appropriate codes (which only Jimmie, having set the machine, would know, and which for prudence's sake he had not communicated to his companions) attempted to interfere with the device's controls, it would become active, and its sickening effects begin to resonate their way around the globe. Violet understood from overheard conversations between Spears' men that a squad of Royal Engineers was already *en route* from Monmouth to examine the machine-shed. None of the supernormals had the slightest idea of where their own mechanic might be now, 'which leaves us,' Percival concluded, 'with a bit of a disaster on our hands if we don't buck our ideas up sharpish.'

There was a silence, as we each digested this horrifying news. After a few seconds, Emily declared, 'This is appalling, Percival. We have to stop it, any way we can.' Her voice betrayed no tremor of fear or self-doubt, and of all her excellent qualities I never admired any more than I did her resolve at that instant.

'You're game for that, then?' Percival grinned. 'Good-o – I hoped you would be. And you, kid?' he asked Freia, giving her a brotherly smile. 'Can you see what you need to do?'

The little blonde girl rolled her eyes and sighed. 'Of *course* I can,' she said, taking Emily's hand in her own. 'Emily, look at Mr Beech.'

The playwright had been doing nothing unusual: indeed, it seemed to me that he had been attempting, with some success, to mimic Violet's trick of effacing himself from all our consciousnesses. He looked highly alarmed at this sudden uncalled-for attention. As Emily turned towards him with a frown, however, she and Freia vanished in a crackle of blue fire.

'Splendid,' said Percival. 'That's that taken care of. Now let's get even with that devil St John Spears.'

It had, I estimated, been scarcely twenty minutes between my first becoming a knowing witness to an act of time-travel and my second. Within that span I had watched two men being knocked unconscious, and discovered that additionally the survival of my species hung in the balance. It was becoming an eventful day, to say the least of it.

Once again Percival set to work with a will, dismantling and cross-wiring the four head-pieces which he had accumulated, both those worn for protection by the soldiers and those imposed by them upon their prisoners. His twelve fingers were intent and deft, and for a while I found it calming just to watch him work. Violet went to sit a short distance away, stubby legs crossed, domed head nodding in concentration. She was attempting to communicate to her fellows in the meeting-hall that they should expect our imminent arrival: forcing the messages through their psychic baffles would be no easy task, she had said, but she believed that she could convey to the brightest of them an inkling of her message.

Lechasseur went to lock Beech and the supine guards inside the store-room which had previously held Freia. The black man had protested when he realised that Emily had been taken on a journey through time, without prior discussion and with only a small child for protection. However, Percival had assured him that her mission was to be a brief one, and Freia's presence on it indispensable, and Lechasseur could hardly dispute the urgency of the matter.

I asked Percival what he was trying to achieve with his tinkering. He said: 'It's obvious enough, to me at least, that this is *Homo peculiar* engineering. Mechanical manipulation of the psychic wavelengths is a long way beyond your people's abilities at present. That wretched Spears must have forced some earlier victim to put together a prototype for him – and bless that supernormal, whoever he was, because he's put one big flaw into the design. It's much too subtle for the likes of Spears' mechanics to spot, but I think, with these four units, I can rig up something that will knock these soldiers altogether for six.'

'Assuming that the terminal doesn't achieve that first,' I said, and Percival grunted in annoyed assent. 'You know, Percival, I really did admire your moral system, and your adherence to it. You were no hypocrite – you would have watched a rational species die at your own hand rather than have betrayed the cause of human progress.'

He said: 'Yes, well. I've been on the receiving end of that kind of thinking now, and it's a chilly place to be.'

I snorted with laughter. 'And yet for a decade I have been in exactly that chilly place, and I've gloried in it! I have idolised you for your unselfishness, your altruism and integrity.'

'My pig-headedness, you mean,' said Percival, and gave a harsh laugh of his own. 'Well, perhaps that's where I really am your better, Erik. I can recognise cant when I hear it, if not (unfortunately) when I spout it myself. If being the "higher type" means anything, it's that we don't any longer *have* to be subject to the will of evolution. We can be *better* than that. What's so noble about evolution, after all? She's cruel, she's arbitrary, she's no respecter of intellect or of compassion – and those who profess to follow her, like poor old Giddy, end up behaving in exactly the same way.

'I've been a very long way away, Clever-clogs, and there's nothing like it for giving you perspective. I saw our present choices quite clearly: to continue to follow evolution's plan in the same old way, or to transcend it. Eradicating the whole species of *Homo sapiens* might seem pretty appealing (and I know you've felt the same at times, so don't you deny it), but it would just be recapitulating all your own errors on a more lavish scale. Those internecine struggles that have held you back for centuries, the brutality, the predatorial behaviour – we can dispense with all of those. And when I say "we", I mean your people as well: all of us who, for now at least, retain our humanity.'

'And sacrifice?' I said, realising how badly I had missed these talks of ours, these miniature symposia where there was scant doubt in either of our minds which of us was the teacher and which the pupil. 'Is that still a noble aspiration?'

He scowled. 'It's necessary sometimes, of course. But to snuff out a unique human spirit for an abstraction, like "progress" or "humanity"? To die or kill for an empty formula would be a shocking waste – never mind the fact that a devotion to one's species is no less self-centred than those absurd loyalties to the tribe that you people profess. Each human life is sacred, Erik.'

I followed his gaze to Violet, now beginning to emerge from her rapture of telepathic communion; and for the first time I thought to wonder who had been the other partner in the generation of that spirit which now grew within her.

3. THE STRUGGLE FOR SURVIVAL

The retaking of the Retreat was as close to being bloodless as such an affair could possibly have come. No doubt an observer who was still expecting, as we all had been during the past few days, to witness a cataclysmic struggle for survival between two noble races would have found the actual events of that noontide comically bathetic. What occurred instead was a more elegant operation, the realisation of a preconceived ideal with the minimum expense of violent effort.

The function of the device which Percival had cannibalised was simply to transmit the harsh, disruptive noises generated by the prisoners' ear-pieces into the soldiers' own. Once it was activated and their concentration thus disrupted, the troops were helpless: their shots went wide, they were unable to communicate with one another, and they did not even succeed in barricading the doors to the meeting-hall. Most of them merely collapsed, clutching ineffectually at their ears, but for the soldiers' own protection the head-sets had not been made such as might easily or quickly be removed. Those few men who did manage to struggle free of them succumbed immediately to the barrage of psychical assaults launched against them by Percival. They could do little to prevent us from invading their stronghold and releasing the prisoners therein.

The one soldier who caused us real trouble was the brutish Krovsky, who (being perhaps reluctant to entrust his sanity to apparatus whose construction he was aware had employed a supernormal's hand) had actually removed his protective head-gear some time earlier. When the attack began he equipped himself with a pistol and a young hostage; but he, too, fell beneath the psychic battery.

The keys to the manacles were obtained and the captives liberated; their former warders were relieved of all their weapons and corralled into a corner of the meeting-space; and I found myself immediately assailed by doubt. Percival had turned the tables very skilfully upon Spears and his men, but what were tables turned in such a situation? Were our current circumstances actually more desirable, or had Emily, Lechasseur and I willingly assisted Percival in defeating the one force which might have averted the evolutionary ascendancy of *Homo peculiar*? Could it be that Percival had duped the three of us with his talk of a moral epiphany? I began to wonder if I had perhaps been a terribly foolish old man.

Such was undoubtedly the opinion of St John Spears. 'For God's sake, Clevedon,' he pleaded with me, 'you've got to see sense. And you –' (this to Lechasseur) '– yes, you, Sam Spade, whoever the Hell you are. I don't care what these creatures have said or done to fool you into taking their side – they've turned you against your own kind, don't you see that? If you'd seen the things I've seen, if you knew what these monsters can do, you'd see it my way, both of you. You fought in the first war, didn't you, Clevedon?' (Of course I had not.) 'And you, boy – did you think the Nazis were worth fighting? Just you wait and see what these freaks do to you!'

I confess that I was deeply troubled. Lechasseur's reaction was, I think, one of contempt.

Suddenly a piping voice said next to me, 'I think that meeting my family must have broken that man's mind,' and Spears gasped in horror as I looked down at the flaxen crown of Freia's head. The little girl was gazing (I thought perhaps sorrowfully) at Spears, who was cowering now: with her were Emily and, as I realised to my surprise, the missing Jimmie.

I turned uneasily away from the unfortunate Colonel as Percival strolled over to us. He said, 'That worked, then. Splendid – though you took your time. Terminal shut down all right?'

'Shut down, dismantled, all the important bits jumped up and down on,' grinned Jimmie. 'They'll not get the old girl working in a hurry.'

A moment's careful thought revealed what must have happened, and this would shortly be confirmed to me by Emily's account. It seemed that when she and Freia had leaped through time together, they had followed the life-trail of Gideon Beech some seven hours into the past, arriving unobserved in the machine-shed just as the playwright had been sabotaging the psychic amplifier. Woman and girl had waited there until Jimmie had turned up; had watched while he had hastily prepared the terminal for use; and had then plucked him out of time with them the instant he had sent his telepathic message, causing what all of us had understood as his baffling vanishment.

To transport a third party on a journey through time was a feat which had not previously appeared possible to Emily, or which at least had never yet been attempted by her and Lechasseur. As we drove back to London later that day, she would speculate that on this occasion it had been Freia's presence, and more precisely the clarity and focus of the child's time-sensitive talent, that had made the thing a practicality.

For now, though, my principal feeling was one of elation at seeing the two time-travellers again. Inevitably, Percival dashed my sensation of relief. 'Jimmie,' he asked now, 'did Freia pass on my other request?'

The mechanical genius grinned again. 'She did indeed. I've given us twenty minutes – hope that's enough. If not, it's too damned late to do anything about it now.'

Alarmed, I asked them, 'Twenty minutes? Twenty minutes until what, precisely?'

At first Percival looked irritated, and then merely long-suffering. 'Well, you know, it's not as if we can keep these men here forever. We can't just let them go, either – they'd be back soon enough, with bigger guns and tanks and helicopters. What we have at present is what they call a "stand-off".'

I was mystified to see that, behind him, most of the other supernormals had begun to arrange themselves into a ring, their hands joined as for a dance. 'Which is why,' he went on, raising his voice to address the crowd of military prisoners as well as our small circle, 'Jimmie has set the Retreat's generator to over-load itself. It's a rather special generator, which produces energy by the direct annihilation of matter. You've got about a quarter of an hour to get as far from here as possible, before a chain reaction takes away a good-sized portion of this hillside.'

'Good God!' I exclaimed. Similar cries of alarm were coming from the men in the corner.

Violet came to stand on Percival's right-hand side, Jimmie at his left. 'Come on then, kid,' said Percival, and lifted an affronted Freia onto his shoulders.

He said to me: 'Don't forget Giddy Beech, and those sentries we locked up. I'm not saying that you *have* to free them, mind. It's up to you. Just … don't forget Giddy, and what his nature has made of him.'

'We're off now, Erik. You'd better look sharp.' Percival took his friends' hands, completing the circle.

There was a blinding flash, blue lightning roared, and all of the peculiar children vanished together into time.

4. EPILOGUE

Since our return to London, my communication with Honoré Lechasseur and Emily Blandish has been both tenuous and sporadic. The lives they lead are complex and unpredictable, and they rarely have the time to spare for social niceties, but Emily at least is kind enough to write to me on occasion.

I understand that their encounter with the supernormal children, including the events at the Retreat and even Lechasseur's bewildering sojourn in the distant future, is to them merely another in the succession of peculiar occurrences which forms the texture of their lives together. For me these matters, and the facts which they have revealed, have become the central concern of my existence, and so, of course, some difference of perspective is unavoidable.

I do know that we each received a visit in early July from St John Spears, accompanied by a government official who carried a sheaf of papers for our autographs. The Colonel blusteringly denounced me as a traitor to the human race, but from what I could gather he is quite relieved to be free at last of the problem of the supernormals. The civil servant merely requested guarantees as to our silence on any number of points, including the actions of Spears' unit and the whole existence of the Hampdenshire Programme. I signed wherever he indicated, without the slightest intention of abiding by his stipulations.

For a time I corresponded with Gideon Beech at his home in

Hertfordshire; but the power of that enormous intellect is waning at last. Despite my earnest efforts to convince him that Percival's people have nothing more to concern them in our time, the ancient playwright abides in terror of their returning to take revenge upon him. He experiences grave difficulty now in distinguishing between his own theatrical fantasias and reality, and I fear that he is not long for this world.

Indeed, I am certain of it. When Honoré Lechasseur related to me the vision which he had been granted by Sanfeil, and in particular when he described the detail of those twin lives, lit by an inner fire not their own, which would emerge unscathed from the Retreat and yet would fade to nothing within the span of a few months; I honestly believe that, in recounting this to me, the good man did not know that he was imparting the news of my own imminent, inevitable demise.

The alternative would be to suppose that he had for some reason formed a dislike of me, which I can scarcely credit to have been the case. He is not an unkind person, merely one who is more suited to acting in and upon the world than he is to analysing it with any kind of intellectual rigour.

I recognise the affliction which ails Beech: for I am myself a sufferer. All of the incidents which followed after the supernormals' exodus into time: the soldiers' panicked evacuation, and our own headlong departure from the doomed Retreat, with Beech and myself crammed into the rear of the Oxford; the light and heat and noise which bathed us all at once as Lechasseur drove frantically, inexpertly, ignoring Emily's shouted advice; even the sheer smooth crater which appeared behind us, swallowing up the farmstead, and at which we stopped to stare in awe; all these I perceived faintly, distantly, through a numbing haze of fear. I felt inside me, rising up inescapably, the anger of my uninvited passenger: the vast and icy displeasure of Sanfeil, the Coming Man. As I have committed to these pages the history of these my life's climactic occurrences, I have felt in me that chilly condemnation, tolerating my completion of this final task before my life shall end.

So be it. It has been a life in which I have striven always to surpass the limitations of my nature, and to urge my fellow men to do likewise.

It has been lived in the firm belief that mankind's present sorry state should be, in his great history to come, the exception rather than the rule; that the human spirit, though it be at present but a feeble glimmering among the dullness of our brute animal lives, will one day be kindled and nurtured till it waxes brighter than the stars; and that there can be no higher cause than the attainment by that spirit of an excellence ever greater, subtler and more vivid. If my ideas as to how these goals might be attained were culpably mistaken, still I cannot credit that I was wrong to extol them.

No more. The history is written, and now perhaps the historian may know peace.

* * *

5th September: It is with an astonishment and exhilaration of which I scarcely thought myself now capable, that I resume my story for one final time. This very night, Percival has returned to visit me.

It happened much as before: I stood outside my study window underneath the stars, and turned my gaze upwards into that dread immensity. The smoke from an early bonfire wafted past me, and its fragrance brought to my mind those ancient inventions of our race, the warning-beacon and the burning-stake: bright symbols of our capacity for salvation and for cruelty. A voice said quietly behind me, 'Hullo, Clever-clogs!' and turning, I saw Percival.

He looked as if he was perhaps in his mid-forties, the wiry hair turned nearly all to grey, the skin creased all around the corners of those large green eyes. 'It's been quite a time, Erik,' he said. 'Longer for me than for you.' He was, he told me, sixty-four years old, and he might look forward to decades, perhaps centuries, of vigorous life. In fact he is my own age to the day, and that is why he chose this time in his own life to come to me tonight. He has seen, done and created many things since we last met: most of these he did not attempt to describe to me, but he tells me that he is now the father of eight children, firstly with Violet, and more recently with another whom I have not met.

'Fatherhood shook me out of my complacency, I don't mind telling you,' he said. 'It's shocking really, looking back on it, that it took a threat to my own family to bring home what I would have done to your whole people. God, what a selfish young monster I was! But I was only human, after all, and that's a quality which is appalling quite as often as it's glorious.'

'"Only human?"' I said. 'Were you no better, then, than that?'

He laughed. 'Oh, that old chestnut. Yes, we're better – but "better at", not "better than". Of course we're better when it comes to telepathy, time-travel and the like. We're better at thinking, and so at all the trivia of art and science and culture. But spiritually better, morally better? No, old man. That was a youthful folly of mine, like so many others.'

He did not tell me where in the reaches of time and space the men and women of his race have made their home, although he hinted that their era will succeed a nearer age when many tyrannies and cataclysms are to be inflicted upon my own species. He spoke of future epochs when the Earth lies fallow, unencumbered by human occupation, while mankind explores his universe: these times will abound in animal and plant life, Percival maintains, and will incorporate a multiplicity of periods when a community may endure unobserved for centuries.

'You've had no trouble from Sanfeil's people, then?' I asked.

He looked shrewdly at me. 'Honoré told you everything, I suppose. No, we've seen no signs of their meddling. Yourself?'

I told him of my fears, my consciousness of the Coming Man's anger spreading within me like a cancer, occluding my perceptions and darkening my spirit. Percival stood silent for a while before saying: 'You know, Erik … Sanfeil insisted that my people must die, so his could live. He said our little microcosm had to be snuffed out, its embers used to kindle the more glorious flame of his own race.

'In those days we all perceived the struggle in terms of my species' survival against yours, *Homo peculiar* versus *Homo sapiens*. But what Sanfeil said made it sound as if his kind was also at stake. My kind had to die, so his could live. And, well, we didn't. We found a way out, instead.'

'But they *will* live,' I said. 'Surely that's inevitable. You and Lechasseur visited their future, after all.'

'My grandchild brought me here,' he told me. 'Freia's grandchild too, as it happens. We cracked the problem of combining the channelling and sensitive genes a generation ago. Some of the brats are regular little time-machines in their own right.' He chuckled. 'Sometimes it causes their parents no end of grief, just tracking them down.

'What I mean to say, old man, is that we've visited a lot of history, and we've learned a few things too about how time works. It's more complicated than you might suppose. When I say that we've seen no signs of Sanfeil's people, I mean *anywhere*. It's as if they never existed.'

'But I feel him,' I said. 'His presence, here inside me.'

'The possibility of him, perhaps,' he said. 'A guilty ghost. He may feel real, Erik, but he has never had the power to command you.

'And even if he had, what then? You can't be always considering the distant future, forever in thrall to some descendant who may never exist, and whose life you couldn't begin to imagine anyway. Do what seems best to you, believe the things you must, and act at all times as if you bear the responsibility for your own life. Even if it turns out not to be the truth, you've honoured your humanity that way, at least. That may be the truest fulfilment that any truly human being can achieve.'

He left me shortly afterward, striding silently away into the night with that familiar loping gait. He did not say, and I did not feel the need to ask, why he had chosen this night of my life on which to visit me.

The smoke of the distant bonfire continued to drift on the wind, and for what seemed the first time, I felt at peace.

AFTERWORD

by the Author, Philip Purser-Hallard

'This book has two authors ...'
Olaf Stapledon, *Last and First Men*, 1930.

William Olaf Stapledon was born in 1886 and died, like Erik Clevedon, in 1950. By profession a philosopher and poet, by inclination a pacifist and socialist, Stapledon became after his death the second most influential figure in British science fiction after HG Wells, with a profound and lasting effect on authors as diverse as CS Lewis, Arthur C Clarke and Brian Aldiss.

I've loved and admired Stapledon's novels since I first read *Last and First Men* at the age of thirteen, and the fascination which his immense and awe-inspiring vision of future history inspired in me has stayed with me ever since. In adolescence, and later as a postgraduate student writing on SF, I devoured nearly all his other fiction: *Star Maker*, *Last Men in London*, *Odd John* and *Sirius*, as well as more obscure works such as *The Flames* and *Darkness and the Light*.

However, like CS Lewis, I admire Stapledon's prodigious imagination more than I do his philosophy. His work has certain flaws which are endemic to the British SF of the inter-War era, together with some disturbing aspects of its own. To twenty-first century sensibilities, the most shocking of these is his espousal of eugenics, which continued for years after the atrocities carried out in the name of that philosophy by the Nazis had become well known. Despite such reservations however, Stapledon remains a magnificent writer of SF, and one of the true geniuses of the genre.

It's my hope, of course, that *Peculiar Lives* can be read separately from Stapledon's work, as a novella in Telos' *Time Hunter* series. Nevertheless, the book is in part a response to a complex, divided man and to his works, and I am greatly indebted to Mr John Stapledon for permission to quote from his father's writings. Although in writing *Peculiar Lives* I have made my character of Erik Clevedon a mouthpiece for many of the ideas expressed in Stapledon's work, it must be noted that Clevedon himself has far more in common with the well-meaning (but often slightly dim) narrators of Stapledon's fictions than with their author. My criticisms of Stapledon's philosophy should not be interpreted as disrespect for his astounding powers of invention: the same is true of George Bernard Shaw, around whom the character of Gideon Beech has been similarly constructed.

Although my primary debt is obviously to Olaf Stapledon himself, there are others whose practical help in preparing the novella must be acknowledged: primarily, of course, David Howe for his assiduous editorial work, and for commissioning what may have seemed at times a worryingly abstruse piece of fiction. Thanks must also go to Helen Angove, Rachel Churcher, Stuart Douglas and Lance Parkin, for criticism of the work in progress; to Daniel O'Mahony for creating the characters of Emily and Honoré, and to the other authors in the series for developing them; to Paul Magrs for the brief mention of one of his characters in Chapter III.3; to Andrew Chapman for advice on copyright law; and to the AP Watt agency on behalf of the Literary Executors of the Estate of HG Wells, for permission to quote from Chapter 5 of *The Time Machine*.

Special thanks are due to my Dad, Terry Hallard, who gave me *Last and First Men* to read in the first place.

Most of all, though, my thanks must go to Bea Purser-Hallard, for her love and her indefatigable support during the writing of this novella, and for providing it with the perfect dedicatee.

ABOUT THE AUTHOR

Philip Purser-Hallard has written science fiction, criticism, comedy sketches and an inordinate number of emails. His first novel, *Of the City of the Saved...*, was published in 2004. His other published works include short fiction in *The Book of the War*, *A Life Worth Living* and *Wildthyme on Top*.

A long-term reader, fan and critic of science fiction, he gained his doctorate from Oxford University by writing on *The Relationship between Creator and Creature in Science Fiction*. This thesis, which examined the work of Olaf Stapledon, George Bernard Shaw and HG Wells among others, earned him the right to put the very appropriate initials 'MA D Phil' after his name.

His comedy has been performed on the Edinburgh Fringe, and he has spoken on 'Science Fiction and the Bible' at the Greenbelt arts festival. He has been employed as a tutor, secretary, church caretaker and researcher for the revised edition of the *Oxford English Dictionary*. He now works as a library assistant in Bristol in South-West England, where he lives with his wife and cats.

His website, which will shortly incorporate some exclusive material relating to *Peculiar Lives*, can be found at www.infinitarian.com.

TIME HUNTER

A range of high-quality, original paperback and limited edition hardback novellas featuring the adventures in time of Honoré Lechasseur. Part mystery, part detective story, part dark fantasy, part science fiction ... these books are guaranteed to enthral fans of good fiction everywhere, and are in the spirit of our acclaimed range of *Doctor Who* Novellas.

ALREADY AVAILABLE

THE WINNING SIDE by LANCE PARKIN

Emily is dead! Killed by an unknown assailant. Honoré and Emily find themselves caught up in a plot reaching from the future to their past, and with their very existence, not to mention the future of the entire world, at stake, can they unravel the mystery before it is too late?
An adventure in time and space.
£7.99 (+ £1.50 UK p&p) Standard p/b ISBN 1-903889-35-9 (pb)

THE TUNNEL AT THE END OF THE LIGHT by STEFAN PETRUCHA

In the heart of post-war London, a bomb is discovered lodged at a disused station between Green Park and Hyde Park Corner. The bomb detonates, and as the dust clears, it becomes apparent that *something* has been awakened. Strange half-human creatures attack the workers at the site, hungrily searching for anything containing sugar ...

Meanwhile, Honoré and Emily are contacted by eccentric poet Randolph Crest, who believes himself to be the target of these subterranean creatures. The ensuing investigation brings Honoré and Emily up against a terrifying force from deep beneath the earth, and one which even with their combined powers, they may have trouble stopping.
An adventure in time and space.
£7.99 (+ £1.50 UK p&p) Standard p/b ISBN 1-903889-37-5 (pb)
£25.00 (+ £1.50 UK p&p) Deluxe h/b ISBN 1-903889-38-3 (hb)

THE CLOCKWORK WOMAN by CLAIRE BOTT

Honoré and Emily find themselves imprisoned in the 19th Century by a celebrated inventor ... but help comes from an unexpected source – a humanoid automaton created by and to give pleasure to its owner. As the trio escape to London, they are unprepared for what awaits them, and at every turn it seems impossible to avert what fate may have in store for the Clockwork Woman.

An adventure in time and space.

£7.99 (+ £1.50 UK p&p) Standard p/b ISBN 1-903889-39-1 (pb)

£25.00 (+ £1.50 UK p&p) Deluxe h/b ISBN 1-903889-40-5 (hb)

KITSUNE by JOHN PAUL CATTON

In the year 2020, Honoré and Emily find themselves thrown into a mystery, as an ice spirit – *Yuki-Onna* – wreaks havoc during the Kyoto Festival, and a haunted funhouse proves to contain more than just paper lanterns and wax dummies. But what does all this have to do with the elegant owner of the Hide and Chic fashion chain ... and to the legendary Chinese fox-spirits, the Kitsune?

An adventure in time and space.

£7.99 (+ £1.50 UK p&p) Standard p/b ISBN 1-903889-41-3 (pb)

£25.00 (+ £1.50 UK p&p) Deluxe h/b ISBN 1-903889-42-1 (hb)

THE SEVERED MAN by GEORGE MANN

What links a clutch of sinister murders in Victorian London, an angel appearing in a Staffordshire village in the 1920s and a small boy running loose around the capital in 1950? When Honoré and Emily encounter a man who appears to have been cut out of time, they think they have the answer. But soon enough they discover that the mystery is only just beginning and that nightmares can turn into reality.

An adventure in time and space.

£7.99 (+ £1.50 UK p&p) Standard p/b ISBN 1-903889-43-X (pb)

£25.00 (+ £1.50 UK p&p) Deluxe h/b ISBN 1-903889-44-8 (hb)

ECHOES by IAIN MCLAUGHLIN & CLAIRE BARTLETT

Echoes of the past ... echoes of the future. Honoré Lechasseur can see the threads that bind the two together, however when he and Emily Blandish find themselves outside the imposing tower-block headquarters of Dragon Industry, both can sense something is wrong.

There are ghosts in the building, and images and echoes of all times pervade the structure. But what is behind this massive contradiction in time, and can Honoré and Emily figure it out before they become trapped themselves …?

An adventure in time and space.

£7.99 (+ £1.50 UK p&p) Standard p/b ISBN 1-903889-45-6 (pb)

£25.00 (+ £1.50 UK p&p) Deluxe h/b ISBN 1-903889-46-4 (hb)

COMING SOON

DEUS LE VOLT by JON DE BURGH MILLER

"Deus Le Volt!" … "God Wills It!" The cry of the first Crusade in 1098, despatched by Pope Urban to free Jerusalem from the Turks. Honoré and Emily are plunged into the middle of the conflict on the trail of what appears to be a time travelling knight. As the siege of Antioch draws to a close, so death haunts the blood-soaked streets … and the Fendahl – a creature that feeds on life itself – is summoned. Honoré and Emily find themselves facing angels and demons in a battle to survive their latest adventure.

An adventure in time and space.

£7.99 (+ £1.50 UK p&p) Standard p/b ISBN 1-903889-49-9 (pb)

£25.00 (+ £1.50 UK p&p) Deluxe h/b ISBN 1-903889-97-9 (hb)

PUB: OCTOBER 2005 (UK)

TIME HUNTER FILM

DAEMOS RISING by DAVID J HOWE, DIRECTED BY KEITH BARNFATHER

Daemos Rising is a sequel to both the *Doctor Who* adventure *The Daemons* and to *Downtime*, an earlier drama featuring the Yeti. It is also a prequel of sorts to Telos Publishing's *Time Hunter* series. It stars Miles Richardson as ex-UNIT operative Douglas Cavendish, and Beverley Cressman as Brigadier Lethbridge-Stewart's daughter Kate. Trapped in an isolated cottage, Cavendish thinks he is seeing ghosts. The only person who might understand and help is Kate Lethbridge-Stewart … but when she arrives, she realises that Cavendish is key in a plot to summon the Daemons back to the Earth. With time running out, Kate discovers that sometimes even the familiar can turn out to be your worst nightmare. Also starring Andrew Wisher, and featuring Ian Richardson as the Narrator. *An adventure in time and space.*

£14.00 (+ £2.50 UK p&p) PAL format R4 DVD

Order direct from Reeltime Pictures, PO Box 23435, London SE26 5WU

HORROR/FANTASY

CAPE WRATH by PAUL FINCH
Death and horror on a deserted Scottish island as an ancient Viking warrior chief returns to life.
£8.00 (+ £1.50 UK p&p) Standard p/b ISBN: 1-903889-60-X

KING OF ALL THE DEAD by STEVE LOCKLEY & PAUL LEWIS
The king of all the dead will have what is his.
£8.00 (+ £1.50 UK p&p) Standard p/b ISBN: 1-903889-61-8

GUARDIAN ANGEL by STEPHANIE BEDWELL-GRIME
Devilish fun as Guardian Angel Porsche Winter loses a soul to the devil …
£9.99 (+ £2.50 UK p&p) Standard p/b ISBN: 1-903889-62-6

FALLEN ANGEL by STEPHANIE BEDWELL-GRIME
Porsche Winter battles she devils on Earth …
£9.99 (+ £2.50 UK p&p) Standard p/b ISBN: 1-903889-69-3

ASPECTS OF A PSYCHOPATH by ALISTAIR LANGSTON
Goes deeper than ever before into the twisted psyche of a serial killer. Horrific, graphic and gripping, this book is not for the squeamish.
£8.00 (+ £1.50 UK p&p) Standard p/b ISBN: 1-903889-63-4

SPECTRE by STEPHEN LAWS
The inseparable Byker Chapter: six boys, one girl, growing up together in the back streets of Newcastle. Now memories are all that Richard Eden has left, and one treasured photograph. But suddenly, inexplicably, the images of his companions start to fade, and as they

vanish, so his friends are found dead and mutilated. Something is stalking the Chapter, picking them off one by one, something connected with their past, and with the girl they used to know. £9.99 (+ £2.50 UK p&p) Standard p/b ISBN: 1-903889-72-3

THE HUMAN ABSTRACT by GEORGE MANN
A future tale of private detectives, AIs, Nanobots, love and death.
£7.99 (+ £1.50 UK p&p) Standard p/b ISBN: 1-903889-65-0

BREATHE by CHRISTOPHER FOWLER
The Office meets *Night of the Living Dead.*
£7.99 (+ £1.50 UK p&p) Standard p/b ISBN: 1-903889-67-7
£25.00 (+ £1.50 UK p&p) Deluxe h/b ISBN: 1-903889-68-5

HOUDINI'S LAST ILLUSION by STEVE SAVILE
Can master illusionist Harry Houdini outwit the dead shades of his past?
£7.99 (+ £1.50 UK p&p) Standard p/b ISBN: 1-903889-66-9

ALICE'S JOURNEY BEYOND THE MOON by R J CARTER
A sequel to the classic Lewis Carroll tales.
£6.99 (+ £1.50 UK p&p) Standard p/b ISBN: 1-903889-76-6
£30.00 (+ £1.50 UK p&p) Deluxe h/b ISBN: 1-903889-77-4

APPROACHING OMEGA by ERIC BROWN
A colonisation mission to Earth runs into problems.
£7.99 (+ £1.50 UK p&p) Standard p/b ISBN: 1-903889-98-7
£30.00 (+ £1.50 UK p&p) Deluxe h/b ISBN: 1-903889-99-5

ANOTHER WAR by SIMON MORDEN
Alien invaders attack the Earth … bringing their god with them.
£7.99 (+ £1.50 UK p&p) Standard p/b ISBN: 1-903889-93-6

VALLEY OF LIGHTS by STEPHEN GALLAGHER
A cop comes up against a body-hopping murderer …
£9.99 (+ £2.50 UK p&p) Standard p/b ISBN: 1-903889-74-X
£30.00 (+ £2.50 UK p&p) Deluxe h/b ISBN: 1-903889-75-8

TV/FILM GUIDES

A DAY IN THE LIFE: THE UNOFFICIAL AND UNAUTHORISED GUIDE TO 24 by KEITH TOPPING

Complete episode guide to the first season of the popular TV show.
£9.99 (+ £2.50 p&p) Standard p/b ISBN: 1-903889-53-7

THE TELEVISION COMPANION: THE UNOFFICIAL AND UNAUTHORISED GUIDE TO DOCTOR WHO by DAVID J HOWE & STEPHEN JAMES WALKER

Complete episode guide to the popular TV show.
£14.99 (+ £4.75 UK p&p) Standard p/b ISBN: 1-903889-51-0

LIBERATION: THE UNOFFICIAL AND UNAUTHORISED GUIDE TO BLAKE'S 7 by ALAN STEVENS & FIONA MOORE

Complete episode guide to the popular TV show.
Featuring a foreword by David Maloney
£9.99 (+ £2.50 UK p&p) Standard p/b ISBN: 1-903889-54-5

HOWE'S TRANSCENDENTAL TOYBOX: SECOND EDITION by DAVID J HOWE & ARNOLD T BLUMBERG

Complete guide to *Doctor Who* Merchandise.
£25.00 (+ £4.75 UK p&p) Standard p/b ISBN: 1-903889-56-1

HOWE'S TRANSCENDENTAL TOYBOX: UPDATE NO. 1: 2003 by DAVID J HOWE & ARNOLD T BLUMBERG

Complete guide to *Doctor Who* Merchandise released in 2003.
£7.99 (+ £1.50 UK p&p) Standard p/b ISBN: 1-903889-57-X

A VAULT OF HORROR by KEITH TOPPING

A Guide to 80 Classic (and not so classic) British Horror Films
£12.99 (+ £4.75 UK p&p) Standard p/b ISBN: 1-903889-58-8

BEAUTIFUL MONSTERS: THE UNOFFICIAL AND UNAUTHORISED GUIDE TO THE ALIEN AND PREDATOR FILMS by DAVID McINTEE

A Guide to the *Alien* and *Predator* Films
£9.99 (+ £2.50 UK p&p) Standard p/b ISBN: 1-903889-94-4

THE HANDBOOK: THE UNOFFICIAL AND UNAUTHORISED GUIDE TO THE PRODUCTION OF DOCTOR WHO by DAVID J HOWE, STEPHEN JAMES WALKER and MARK STAMMERS

Complete guide to the making of *Doctor Who*.
£14.99 (+ £4.75 UK p&p) Standard p/b ISBN: 1-903889-59-6
£30.00 (+ £4.75 UK p&p) Deluxe h/b ISBN: 1-903889-96-0

HANK JANSON

Classic pulp crime thrillers from the 1940s and 1950s.

TORMENT by HANK JANSON
£9.99 (+ £1.50 UK p&p) Standard p/b ISBN: 1-903889-80-4

WOMEN HATE TILL DEATH by HANK JANSON
£9.99 (+ £1.50 UK p&p) Standard p/b ISBN: 1-903889-81-2

SOME LOOK BETTER DEAD by HANK JANSON
£9.99 (+ £1.50 UK p&p) Standard p/b ISBN: 1-903889-82-0

SKIRTS BRING ME SORROW by HANK JANSON
£9.99 (+ £1.50 UK p&p) Standard p/b ISBN: 1-903889-83-9

WHEN DAMES GET TOUGH by HANK JANSON
£9.99 (+ £1.50 UK p&p) Standard p/b ISBN: 1-903889-85-5

ACCUSED by HANK JANSON
£9.99 (+ £1.50 UK p&p) Standard p/b ISBN: 1-903889-86-3

KILLER by HANK JANSON
£9.99 (+ £1.50 UK p&p) Standard p/b ISBN: 1-903889-87-1

FRAILS CAN BE SO TOUGH by HANK JANSON
£9.99 (+ £1.50 UK p&p) Standard p/b ISBN: 1-903889-88-X

BROADS DON'T SCARE EASY by HANK JANSON
£9.99 (+ £1.50 UK p&p) Standard p/b ISBN: 1-903889-89-8

KILL HER IF YOU CAN by HANK JANSON
£9.99 (+ £1.50 UK p&p) Standard p/b ISBN: 1-903889-90-1

THE TRIALS OF HANK JANSON by STEVE HOLLAND
£12.99 (+ £2.50 UK p&p) Standard p/b ISBN: 1-903889-84-7

The prices shown are correct at time of going to press. However, the publishers reserve the right to increase prices from those previously advertised without prior notice.

TELOS PUBLISHING
c/o Beech House, Chapel Lane, Moulton, Cheshire, CW9 8PQ, England
Email: orders@telos.co.uk
Web: www.telos.co.uk

To order copies of any Telos books, please visit our website where there are full details of all titles and facilities for worldwide credit card online ordering, or send a cheque or postal order (UK only) for the appropriate amount (including postage and packing), together with details of the book(s) you require, plus your name and address to the above address. Overseas readers please send two international reply coupons for details of prices and postage rates.